MONTANA MAVERICKS

Welcome to Big Sky Country, home of the Montana Mavericks! Where free-spirited men and women discover love on the range.

LASSOING LOVE

After years away, some of Bronco's most memorable sons and daughters have returned to the ranch seeking a fresh start. But there are some bumps along the road to redemption. Expect the unexpected as lonesome cowboys (and cowgirls) discover if they've got what it takes to grab that second chance!

They were two kids who were wild about each other, but Charlotte knew she wasn't ready to be a wife. She was only seventeen when she left her beloved Billy behind—at the altar! Now she's an esteemed marine biologist who has traveled the world, and Billy is a divorced dad of three who never left Bronco. Is their Christmas reunion just a trip down memory lane—or a chance to walk hand in hand into the future?

Dear Reader,

It's said that there's no place like home for the holidays, but Charlotte Taylor hasn't returned to Bronco for everything merry and bright, but to meet Merry—her sister's baby girl! As it turns out, though, the marine biologist has some time on her hands as she waits for a research grant to come through, and she decides to spend it catching up with her family and getting reacquainted with old friends.

Recently divorced Billy Abernathy isn't feeling the holiday spirit this year, though he's trying hard to fake it for the benefit of his three kids. Coming face-to-face with his runaway bride from twenty years ago does absolutely nothing to improve his mood. In fact, seeing her again only makes him feel worse about his failed marriage, because he knows he never loved his wife the way he once loved Charlotte.

But circumstances (and perhaps a little bit of holiday magic) conspire to throw Charlotte and Billy together. Gradually old wounds are healed and a forgotten spark is reignited, forcing the long-ago high school sweethearts to consider that it might be time to give first love a second chance...

I hope you enjoy this visit to Bronco, Montana, and Charlotte and Billy's story.

Happy reading and happy holidays!

Enjoy,

Brenda xo

A Maverick's
Holiday
Homecoming

———

BRENDA HARLEN

HARLEQUIN
SPECIAL
EDITION

Special thanks and acknowledgment are given to Brenda Harlen for her contribution to the Montana Mavericks: Lassoing Love miniseries.

Recycling programs
for this product may
not exist in your area.

ISBN-13: 978-1-335-59438-9

A Maverick's Holiday Homecoming

Copyright © 2023 by Harlequin Enterprises ULC

For questions and comments about the quality of this book, please contact us at CustomerService@Harlequin.com.

Harlequin Enterprises ULC
22 Adelaide St. West, 41st Floor
Toronto, Ontario M5H 4E3, Canada
www.Harlequin.com

Printed in U.S.A.

Brenda Harlen is a former attorney who once had the privilege of appearing before the Supreme Court of Canada. The practice of law taught her a lot about the world and reinforced her determination to become a writer—because in fiction, she could promise a happy ending! Now she is an award-winning, RITA® Award–nominated, nationally bestselling author of more than fifty titles for Harlequin. You can keep up-to-date with Brenda on Facebook and Twitter, or through her website, brendaharlen.com.

Books by Brenda Harlen

Harlequin Special Edition

Match Made in Haven

The Rancher's Promise
The Chef's Surprise Baby
Captivated by the Cowgirl
Countdown to Christmas
Her Not-So-Little Secret
The Rancher's Christmas Reunion

Montana Mavericks: Brothers & Broncos

The Maverick's Christmas Secret

Montana Mavericks:
The Real Cowboys of Bronco Heights

Dreaming of a Christmas Cowboy

Montana Mavericks: What Happened to Beatrix?

A Cowboy's Christmas Carol

Montana Mavericks: Lassoing Love

A Maverick's Holiday Homecoming

Visit the Author Profile page
at Harlequin.com for more titles.

For Sharon & Ken—who introduced me
to the Bahamas (and the dolphins!)

Prologue

She couldn't breathe.

Charlotte Taylor put her hands on hips draped in floral lace over ivory satin and desperately tried to draw air into her lungs. Her fingers curled into fists, clutching the delicate fabric as she envisioned tearing it from her body. The fitted bodice, embellished with thousands of shimmery glass beads, felt too tight, like a vise around her ribs. The skirt, with its long train, was both cumbersome and heavy.

Or maybe it was the weight of so many expectations that she felt pressing down on her.

A breeze blew through the courtyard behind the church, making her veil flutter.

She shoved it away from her face.

Everyone—from her grandmother to the seamstress at the bridal salon—had told her that a bride's wedding day was the happiest day of her life, so why wasn't her heart filled with light and joy? Why did the prospect of walking down the aisle fill her with dread rather than anticipation? Why did the idea of exchanging vows feel like the end of her life rather than the beginning?

Her parents, Thaddeus and Imogen Taylor, had spared no expense when it came to their eldest daughter's wedding. Not because she needed a couture gown from Italy or a five-tier wedding cake designed by a Parisian pastry chef or a mountain of flowers flown in from Texas, but because the residents of Bronco, Montana, expected the richest family in town to pull out all the stops for the nuptials of one of their own.

Over the sounds of birds chirping and leaves rustling in the breeze, she could hear guests gathering in the chapel, talking and laughing.

Because a wedding was a day of celebration—unless you were a seventeen-year-old bride.

"Charlotte?"

She jolted at the sound of his voice—almost as familiar to her as her own.

She'd known Billy Abernathy most of her life and had loved him almost as long, and her heart pinched when she looked at him now.

He was so handsome in his suit. Tall and broad-shouldered. From the back, he could easily be mistaken for a man. But from the front, he was obviously still a boy. Charlotte doubted if he'd even had to shave for the occasion, as he'd done so for their high school graduation, three days earlier.

He'd had his hair trimmed, though. No doubt at his

mother's insistence, because he knew that Charlotte preferred when his dark blond hair was long enough to curl at the ends.

His moss-green eyes were focused on her now, his expression far too serious for someone so young.

Of course, they were both young.

Too young.

Why did nobody else see what seemed so obvious to her?

"What are you doing out here?" Billy asked, sounding concerned.

"I just needed some air," she told him.

It was the truth—if only a small part of it.

"But *you* shouldn't be out here," she felt compelled to protest. "It's bad luck for the groom to see the bride before the ceremony."

"That old superstition," he scoffed, gently uncurling her fingers from her skirt to link them with his own. His lips curved as his gaze skimmed over her. "You take my breath away, Char."

"That seems to be a common problem today," she muttered.

His handsome brow furrowed. "Huh?"

"It's nothing."

"You've got something on your mind," he guessed.

"So many things," she admitted.

"Anything you want to talk about?"

She shook her head. "No. Not now."

She'd been trying to talk to him for weeks—and to her parents, too—but no one wanted to hear what she had to say. Her concerns about the big day were easily dismissed as pre-wedding jitters and she was reminded that she and Billy had been preparing for this day since kindergarten.

Of course, the vows they'd exchanged in their mock wedding on the playground when they were five years old hadn't been anything more than a promise to always be friends and to share any Little Debbie snack cakes they might find in their lunchboxes.

But they weren't kids anymore, and this time, it was for real. Forever.

Oh God, now she really couldn't breathe.

Then Billy's lips were on hers and the panic—and everything else—faded away.

A long minute later, he drew back.

"What…why…"

"You were hyperventilating," he explained. "And it was the easiest way I could think of to slow your breathing."

"You don't carry a paper bag around with you?"

He smiled the familiar smile that she knew would remain etched in her mind—and her heart—forever.

"I don't think that's necessary. You're okay. Just some pre-wedding jitters, I think."

She nodded, because she knew there was no way she was going to convince him any differently at this late stage of the game.

He squeezed her hands gently, reassuringly. "You know I love you, don't you?"

"And I love you," she told him.

Because it was true.

She loved him with everything in her heart and her soul—but she wasn't ready to be anyone's wife.

"Should I tell your dad that you'll be right in?" he asked.

Charlotte nodded again.

He released her hands, gave her another smile, then turned and walked back into the church.

She watched as the door closed behind him, then she turned in the opposite direction and started to run—not an easy task in a long dress and high heels. So she hiked up the skirt and kicked off her shoes and wondered if this was how Cinderella felt making a mad dash from the ball at midnight.

But unlike the princess in the fairy tale, Charlotte wasn't looking for ever after—she was still waiting for her life to begin.

Chapter One

Twenty years later

Returning to Bronco, Montana, always felt strange to Charlotte Taylor—and it was no less so this time despite being her second visit in two weeks. The first visit had been to celebrate Thanksgiving with her family—and now she was back to meet her baby sister's baby girl.

Eloise was the youngest of the six Taylor siblings but the first to become a parent. And though Thaddeus had been grumbling about Eloise's status (unmarried and pregnant!) at Thanksgiving, all was forgiven now that they'd met the little bundle of joy. In fact, Thad and Imogen had apparently been strutting proudly around town, showing off photos of Merry—"our first grandchild"—to anyone who paused long enough to ask about the new baby. (As reported by Cassidy Taylor—

the owner of Bronco Java and Juice and her cousin-in-law through marriage—when Charlotte stopped in for a jolt of caffeine before making her way to the Heights Hotel, where Eloise was currently living with her baby and Dante Sanchez.)

It stung, more than a little, to discover that everyone else had apparently forgotten the baby that Charlotte had carried in her womb for a few short weeks. Especially when that baby had been the reason for the shotgun wedding Thaddeus and Imogen had been so eager to plan. Of course, her parents and Billy's had been convinced of the benefits of a merger between their families—the Abernathys being the second wealthiest ranching dynasty in Bronco—which was why, when she'd suffered a miscarriage, no one wanted to call off the wedding.

No one except Charlotte.

But that was ancient history.

And while Eloise had also committed the sin (in the eyes of their father) of conceiving a child outside of wedlock, there had been no shotgun wedding for her.

That's not to say there wouldn't have been if Eloise had given Thaddeus even a hint about the identity of her baby's father. But she'd been smart enough not to do so, and strong enough to make her own choices about what she wanted for her future and her baby's.

And apparently that included Dante Sanchez.

The man had been a stranger to Eloise when she got into his car to escape an awkward family gathering, but now, after a whirlwind romance, her sister had proclaimed him to be the love of her life.

Charlotte stopped at the front desk to collect the key card her sister had promised to leave for her. She hadn't been sure what time she would arrive and the new mom had no idea if she might be nursing or changing the baby and didn't want her sister having to stand out in the hall, waiting.

Still, Charlotte knocked first—and the door immediately opened from the other side.

"You're here!" Eloise threw her arms around her. "But why did you knock? Didn't you get the key from downstairs?"

Charlotte hugged her back, as best as she could manage with her hands full. "I got the key," she confirmed. "I just didn't want to come barging in."

"I want you to barge in—anytime," her sister said, dragging her over the threshold. "In fact, I'm hoping you'll spend a lot of time here with us while you're in Bronco for the holidays."

"We'll figure something out." She set her bags on the floor, then removed her coat and boots.

Eloise took her coat to put it in the small closet, frowning as she draped it over a hanger. "Please tell me you have something warmer than this."

"I don't need a down-filled parka in the Bahamas."

"Maybe not," her sister allowed. "But you're going to wish you had one here."

"I'm trusting that Mom has an extra coat—or four or five—that I can borrow while I'm in town."

"And probably boots, too," Eloise said. "Because you're going to need warmer ones than what you were wearing."

"No doubt. But I didn't come here to talk about the weather," Charlotte said. "I came to see my little sister— the new mama. And I'd love a peek at her gorgeous baby, too."

"You haven't seen her yet, so how can you be sure she's gorgeous?"

"Because she's yours," Charlotte said simply.

The new mom's eyes filled with tears.

"I'm sorry."

Eloise managed a watery smile. "Why are you sorry?"

"Because I made you cry."

"Everything makes me cry these days," her sister warned. "Thankfully, Dante hasn't been scared away by my tears."

"Speaking of your new man—is he here?"

Eloise shook her head. "He's at school until three o'clock."

"School?" she echoed cautiously.

Her sister laughed. "He's not a student, he's a teacher of third grade at Bronco Valley Elementary."

"That's a relief," Charlotte said, laughing with her. "Because I'm really looking forward to meeting him."

"He's eager to meet you, too," Eloise assured her, tucking her arm through her sister's and leading her into the bedroom. "But right now, come and meet Merry."

"Did I mention in my text message how much I love her name?"

"You did," the new mom confirmed, her voice now a whisper as she drew Charlotte closer to the bassinet in which the newborn was sleeping.

"Ohmygod." Charlotte had to blink the tears from

her eyes to focus on the baby. Not that she could see much, as the infant was swaddled in a blanket with knitted mittens on her hands and a matching cap on her head. But her face was relaxed in sleep, her features perfectly symmetrical—her brows and lashes dark, her nose a tiny little button, her mouth the shape of a Cupid's bow. "She's so tiny."

"You'd have a different opinion if you'd had to push her out of your body," Eloise remarked dryly.

Charlotte smiled. "And so perfect."

"I'm not going to disagree with that."

Gazing down at her infant niece, Charlotte felt her heart fill with love—and a subtle pang of longing. "Do you spend hours every day just staring at her?"

"It's only been a couple of days," Eloise reminded her sister. "But yes."

"Can I call dibs so I get to hold her as soon as she wakes up?"

"She's going to be hungry when she wakes up."

"Okay, I call dibs for after you've fed her," Charlotte amended. "And changed her."

Eloise chuckled softly as she drew her sister away from the bassinet and back to the living room, where they could talk freely without having to worry about waking the baby.

"Can I get you anything to eat or drink?" she offered.

"No, you need to sit and relax—and let me know if I can get you anything," Charlotte said.

"Sitting and relaxing is all I've been doing since I came home from the hospital yesterday."

"I'm happy to hear that." She settled onto the opposite end of the sofa from her sister and took a minute to survey the main living area of the hotel suite, admiring the contemporary décor and the comfortable looking furnishings. "This is a really nice place."

"Thank you," Eloise said, with more emphasis than was warranted.

"Someone doesn't like it?" Charlotte guessed.

Her sister sighed. "Dante," she confided. "Well, he likes the hotel just fine—because what's not to like? But he's eager for us to move into a house."

"I have to admit, I'm still a little surprised that you decided to move back to Bronco," she told her sister.

It was hardly a secret that Eloise had been furious with their father for refusing to give her any real responsibility in the family business, her education and obvious capabilities notwithstanding. So she'd walked out of her office, packed her belongings, and moved out of town.

After adding an MBA from Columbia to her résumé, she'd built her own company from the ground up. In the four years that had passed since then, Taylor Marketing had acquired wide range of clients—most of them businesses run by women—and was hugely successful.

Eloise shrugged. "I'm lucky that I can do my work almost anywhere and, as my pregnancy progressed, I realized that I wanted my baby to grow up with family."

"She's going to be so spoiled."

"I know it," the new mom admitted. "She already has more outfits than she'll be able to wear before she outgrows them."

"Which is why I got her a gift card for the Hey, Baby store in Bronco Heights," Charlotte said.

"That's absolutely perfect. But really, you didn't need to get anything."

"I wanted to. And though I'm sure Merry already has a mountain of toys as well as clothes, I couldn't resist this," Charlotte said, retrieving a gift bag decorated with pastel pink swirls and stuffed with pink tissue paper from where she'd left it near the door.

Her sister pulled out the paper, then the fluffy white teddy bear with a pink nose and floral patches on its ears and paws.

"I can't believe it—it looks just like Tubby," Eloise said, naming her favorite childhood teddy bear.

Charlotte had tried to teach her little sister to say "teddy" but the best the two-year-old could manage at the time was "tubby," and so that had become the toy's name.

"I thought so, too," she said. "Which is why I had to buy it."

"Merry's going to love it," Eloise said confidently.

Conversation moved on to other topics while the baby continued to sleep—including more details about Eloise's first meeting with Dante and the immediate and unexpected attraction that led to them quickly falling in love. It turned out there were various other connections between the Taylor and the Sanchez families, too, which her sister pointed out.

Eloise nursed and changed the baby when she woke up from her nap, then, as promised, passed her to Charlotte's waiting arms.

Merry yawned—a huge yawn for such a little one—and blinked her big blue eyes at her aunt.

"She has your eyes," Charlotte told her sister.

"My eyes are brown," Eloise pointed out.

"Hers will be, too," she predicted. "But I wasn't referring to the color so much as the shape. And those lashes are definitely a gift from her mama."

It was fascinating to look at the baby and see traces of Eloise in her features. At the same time, it made Charlotte wonder what features she and Billy might have passed on to their child.

She hadn't given much thought to that question when she was seventeen, because she'd been too busy freaking out about the fact that she was going to be a teenage mother. And then, just when she'd started to accept her new reality, it changed again, and the tiny life she and Billy had created together was gone.

Thinking about that baby now, she felt a familiar pinch in her heart. But she shook off her melancholy, reminding herself that she had much to be grateful for—including an exciting career as a marine biologist that allowed her to travel to some of the most beautiful places on earth to study dolphins and their natural habitat.

Of course, all that travel for work had kept her away from Montana for a lot of years, leading Thaddeus to warn—in the ominous tone of voice he only ever used with his daughters—that she was going to regret the choices she'd made. Because, in his mind, prioritizing career over family was perfectly acceptable for a man (and maybe even expected) but wholly unnatural for a woman.

Charlotte didn't agree with her father (she rarely

did!), though she couldn't deny that she'd focused on her career above all else. Because when she'd left Bronco twenty years earlier, she'd not only needed something to fill the emptiness in her heart but also to pay her rent and put food on her table.

She hadn't had a real plan when she walked out of her wedding. Even when she threw her suitcases (already packed, because she was expected to move in with her husband after the exchange of vows) into the trunk of her SUV, she wasn't sure where she wanted to go. She'd just started driving and found herself headed west. Eventually she made her way to Seattle, where she got a job bussing tables at a restaurant near the waterfront.

It was summer—the height of tourist season—so the restaurant was busy and tips were good, but after a few weeks in a budget motel in a questionable part of town, she was happy to accept the offer of a coworker to share her one-bedroom apartment and her rent. In addition to working at the restaurant, Marissa was a student at the nearby University of Washington, studying marine biology, and her roommate's enthusiasm for the subject was so infectious that Charlotte found herself wanting to study it, too.

She had no regrets about the path she'd taken, and she'd never felt anything but fulfilled in her career. In fact, the only times she'd ever experienced any hints of regret were on the rare occasions that she returned to Bronco. Walking along the streets she remembered walking hand in hand with Billy, she couldn't help but wonder *what if.*

But there was nothing to be gained from second-guessing the choices she'd made. Yes, there had been a time when she'd truly believed that her future was with Billy Abernathy, but she'd ultimately turned down a different path. And, eventually, so had he. Her abandoned groom got his happy ending, marrying a girl he fell in love with at college and having three children with her.

Again, she pushed the memories out of her mind to focus on her sister and her baby girl. Though Eloise had been back in Bronco less than two months herself, it was apparently long enough to have caught up on all the local gossip, and she readily passed on the juiciest tidbits to her sister. Charlotte couldn't help but notice, though, that Eloise made absolutely no mention of anything happening with the Abernathy family.

"You didn't tell me that Jace is adopting the baby he delivered a few months back—or that he's engaged to Tamara Hanson," she noted.

"Oh, that's old news," Eloise said dismissively.

"Is that really the reason?" Charlotte pressed. "Or are you afraid that mentioning the Abernathys will make me think of Billy?"

"Does it?" her sister asked.

"Of course," she admitted. "We were friends for most of our lives, but it's been twenty years since I left town and I can assure you that I'm no longer carrying a torch for my onetime fiancé."

"I've always wondered why you agreed to marry Billy in the first place when it quickly became apparent that you didn't want to walk down the aisle."

"You're right. I never should have agreed to marry

him, but I was facing a lot of pressure. More from Mom and Dad than from Billy," she confided. "And I wasn't strong enough to make them listen to me when I tried to say no."

"But why were they pressuring you to get married at such a young age?" Eloise wondered aloud. "I mean, I'm sure they thought a merger between the Taylors and Abernathys would be beneficial to Taylor Beef, but..." She trailed off, her eyes widening as the answer came to her. "You were pregnant."

Though it wasn't a question, Charlotte nodded.

"How did I not know?"

"You were ten years old," she reminded her sister. "How could you know? Mom and Dad certainly weren't going to tell you that your big sister had gotten pregnant out of wedlock."

"Instead, they rushed you toward a marriage you weren't ready for," Eloise realized.

"I did love Billy, and I really thought we'd get married someday—but someday was supposed to be after we'd both gone to college and experienced some of what the world had to offer. Instead, I got pregnant, and that seemed to seal my fate to follow in our mother's footsteps—married to a rancher and having his babies.

"And then... I lost the baby." Even after so many years, it wasn't easy to say the words aloud and it wasn't possible to think about the miscarriage without wondering what might have been. "Less than two weeks after I found out I was pregnant, I suddenly wasn't. But the wedding plans were already in motion and no one wanted to change them."

"No one but you," her sister guessed.

Charlotte nodded again. "I know I should have handled the situation differently. I should have been honest with Billy about what I wanted—and didn't want. But, in the end, he got the wife and family he dreamed of, and… I'm happy for him. Sincerely."

"Yeah, well, about that," Eloise said.

"What *about that*?" Charlotte prompted.

"Apparently Jane—Billy's wife—walked out on her husband and kids. They're getting a divorce."

Chapter Two

This probably wasn't one of his best ideas, Billy Abernathy acknowledged, as he stared into the amber liquid in his glass. But he'd needed to get out of the house—which was too damn quiet and empty without his kids, who were having dinner with their mom, per the terms of the custody agreement—and found himself pulling into the parking lot of Doug's Bar without consciously having driven in that direction.

His beer glass was half empty—or half full, depending on one's perspective, he acknowledged—when his brother Theo straddled the vacant stool beside him, at the opposite end of the bar from the infamous Death Seat.

"What's up with you?" Theo asked.

"Why does anything need to be up?" Billy challenged.

"Because you're sitting in a bar, drinking by yourself, on a Wednesday night."

Doug, working behind the bar of his namesake establishment, set a draft in front of Theo.

"Are you planning to drink that?" Billy asked.

"Of course," his brother confirmed, lifting the glass.

"Then I'm not drinking by myself, am I?"

Theo swallowed a mouthful of beer. "Seriously, bro—what's going on?"

Billy stared into his own glass for another minute, as if the answers to the universe—or at least a cure for his melancholy—might be found there.

"The divorce decree came in the mail today," he finally confided. "It's officially over now. Done."

"Was it really a big surprise?"

"No," he admitted. Because how could it be when his wife had been living with Henri for the past several months? "But I still thought—*hoped*—that our family meant more to her than a new boyfriend. Even when she sent the papers, even when I signed them, I was sure she'd change her mind."

"And if she'd changed her mind—would you have taken her back?"

"I would have at least considered it." And he wasn't ashamed of the fact. "I would have done anything to prevent my family from being torn apart."

"You're thinking about the kids," Theo realized.

"Of course, I'm thinking about the kids. This has been so hard on all of them. Branson, who's always been a good student, is suddenly getting in trouble in school. Nicky used to be so outgoing, but now he just wants to stay in his room and play video games. He doesn't even want to hang out with his friends. And

Jill…my Jilly Bean, my sweet little girl, is suddenly having mood swings and tantrums the likes of which I never could have imagined."

"It's a big change," Theo acknowledged. "But they'll get through this—because they've got you."

He snorted. "If I was such a prize, Jane wouldn't have left me."

"Forget about Jane. She's your ex-wife now," his brother reminded him. "But Branson, Nicky and Jill are still your kids and you're still their father. The man who's always been there for them—and who will always be there for them."

Billy swallowed a mouthful of beer before he ventured to ask, "Do you think it's my fault?"

"Do I think *what's* your fault?" Theo said cautiously.

"The failure of my marriage."

"Did you cheat on her?"

"No."

"Then I'm going to give the same answer."

"I didn't cheat," he reiterated. "But maybe I didn't love her enough."

"Did you fall into the married couples' trap of only on Saturday nights?"

Billy rolled his eyes. "I wasn't referring to the frequency of—"

"I get what you weren't referring to," Theo said, holding up a hand to cut off his explanation. "So why don't you tell me what you were referring to."

"When I asked Jane to marry me, I loved her—as much as I could considering that I'd given my heart away years earlier and had it shattered into pieces when Charlotte left me at the altar."

"How many of those have you had?" his brother asked, gesturing to Billy's glass of beer.

"Two." He frowned. "Maybe three."

Theo waved Doug over and ordered chili cheese nachos.

"I could go for some nachos," he said, nodding his head as his brother placed the order.

"I figured you could use something to soak up the beer," Theo said, lifting his own glass. "And that stuff about Charlotte—ancient history. I doubt very much that the wedding-that-never-happened had anything to do with the breakdown of your marriage to Jane."

"Well, I'm not so sure." Billy drained the last mouthful of beer from his glass and gestured to the bartender for another.

"You got a ride home?" Doug asked. Because the man might be in the business of selling beer, but he had no tolerance for drinking and driving.

"I've got him," Theo promised.

Billy didn't claim that he could drive himself, because he knew that wasn't a good idea. Besides, it was hardly out of Theo's way to take him, as they both had their own homes on the Bonnie B. Though Theo lived alone in his, relishing his bachelor lifestyle as much as his own space.

The bartender nodded and tipped another glass under the tap.

"When Jane told me that she'd fallen in love with Henri, she said that she always knew I didn't love her as much as she loved me. She said that she'd gone into our marriage with her eyes open, believing she loved me enough to make our marriage work. But as the kids got older and grew more independent, she began to feel less fulfilled with her life.

"That's when she started taking French classes—which is where she met Henri." Henri Rousseau was from France, teaching French at the local community college in nearby Wonderstone Ridge.

"Sounds to me like she was just looking for an excuse to justify her infidelity," Theo said.

"I asked her—where are you ever going to use French in Bronco? Do you know what she said?"

"In bed with my French teacher?"

Billy scowled at him.

"Sorry," Theo apologized. "Bad joke."

"She said she'd always dreamed of going to Paris someday. And maybe, now that the kids were older, we could plan a romantic getaway—just the two of us.

"That's when I realized that we hadn't taken a trip anywhere, just the two of us, since our honeymoon—and that was only to Little Bighorn."

"Oh, man. Don't tell me you were actually looking into trips to Paris."

"Okay," Billy said. "I'll only tell you that I cleared all flight and hotel searches from my browser history as soon as I found out she was sleeping with her French teacher."

Theo swore.

Billy nodded and lifted his glass again.

"Hey, there." A couple of young women—one blonde,

one brunette—both in tight sweaters and tighter jeans sidled up to the bar, smiling and fluttering obviously fake eyelashes. "You cowboys want some company?"

"Not tonight, ladies," Theo said regretfully.

"Speak for yourself," Billy told him, grateful for any distraction that might brighten his dark mood.

The brunette touched a hand to his arm, her smile widening.

He tried to smile back, but he wasn't really feeling it.

"What brings you out to Doug's tonight?" he asked instead.

It was the blonde who spoke again, responding to his question. "We're celebrating Giselle's birthday."

"I'm Giselle," the brunette said, in a heavily accented tone, as she stroked a finger tipped with a glossy red nail down his forearm.

"French?" Billy guessed.

She smiled. *"Mais, oui."*

Theo snorted.

Billy swore.

The two women exchanged puzzled glances.

"How did you even find this place?" Theo asked. "Not a lot of tourists stumble into Doug's."

"Google." It was Giselle's companion who answered the question. "We were looking for a cowboy bar and this one was the closest."

"Are you even old enough to drink?" Billy asked dubiously.

"I am twenty-two," Giselle said proudly. "Charley is twenty-four."

"Charley?" Theo said.

"A nickname," the blonde admitted. "My real name's Charlotte."

Billy choked on a mouthful of beer.

Theo snorted again as he thumped his brother on the back.

"This is so *not* happening," Billy said, when he'd stopped sputtering and could speak again.

Now Giselle frowned. *"Je ne comprends pas."* She looked to her friend. "I do not…understand?"

"I don't understand, either," Charley said.

"Unfortunately, my brother has just been reminded of all the mistakes he's made in his life," Theo chimed in.

"Not all of them," Billy said. "Just the biggest ones."

Theo waved Doug over again. "Give the ladies a round of whatever they're drinking and put it on my tab."

"Merci," Giselle said, apparently having no difficulty comprehending the offer of a free drink.

Of course, Doug carded them before pouring their drinks.

They asked for red wine. Not cabernet sauvignon or merlot—simply red wine, because that's how it was listed on the menu. Which was why you didn't go to Doug's and order wine.

Not that Billy was a connoisseur, but he knew enough about wine to know not to order it in a bar that catered to cowboys.

Giselle and Charley seemed happy enough, though, and they thanked Theo for their drinks before moving along.

"Maybe we should join them," Billy said, watching as they seated themselves at an empty table.

"You don't want to do that," Theo said. "Plus, we've got nachos coming."

As if on cue, Doug set a heaping plate of chips laden with chili and cheese on the bar between them.

"I *should* want to do that," Billy said. "And I should be celebrating, too, because I'm now finally unshackled after more than eighteen years of marriage."

"Now you're ready to celebrate what you were crying about half an hour ago?" Theo asked dubiously.

"I wasn't crying."

"Close enough."

"The point is, I wouldn't be breaking any vows if I decided that I wanted to take an attractive woman home with me."

"Are you referring to the home where you live with your three kids?"

"Yeah, I guess that's not happening," Billy admitted. "But we could go back to her place."

Theo nodded his thanks to the bartender for the glass of Coke, as he was obviously the designated driver tonight. "If she has a place of her own."

"Or the Ponderosa Motel."

"The rooms are clean but the walls are thin," Theo noted.

Billy sighed. "I guess it's just you and me tonight, bro."

"Lucky me."

He ignored his brother's sarcasm and shoved another nacho in his mouth.

* * *

Billy woke up with a dry mouth and a pounding head.

Reluctantly peeling his eyes open, he squinted at the clock on his bedside table.

7:10.

He swore—then winced at the sound of his own voice.

Obviously he'd forgotten to set his alarm.

Most ranchers were up before the sun, and that had been Billy's routine, too, prior to his wife walking out on her family. Luckily, he worked the Bonnie B with his father and his siblings, and they hadn't grumbled too much about Billy wanting to see his kids off to school before starting his day.

He dragged his body out of bed now and quickly dressed, then headed to the kitchen for a much-needed jolt of caffeine. He had a programmable machine, which meant that coffee should be waiting for him—so long as he'd remembered to set it up the night before.

"If you don't hurry up, you're gonna miss your bus," he heard Branson warning his sister.

"I can't go to school today," Jill said.

"What are you gonna do—hang around here all day to see if Dad comes back?" Nicky challenged.

"Whoa!" Billy said, interrupting their conversation as he stepped through the doorway. "Dad's right here."

"Daddy!" Jill's eyes filled with tears as she launched herself into his arms.

"What's going on? Where did you think I was?" he asked, grateful for his daughter's hug, as they were few and far between these days.

"Your truck's not in the driveway."

There was hurt along with the accusation in Branson's voice, and Billy realized that the kids had interpreted the missing vehicle as a sign that he'd left them—like their mother had done.

He swore again—but only in his head this time.

"I had a couple beers at Doug's last night," he admitted. "Uncle Theo brought me home."

Jill drew back, looking at him through narrowed eyes. "Are you...*hungover*?"

He made his way to the blessedly full coffeepot, reaching into the cupboard above it for a mug. "That would explain the pounding in my head."

"You were drinking at Doug's on a Wednesday night?" His daughter sounded scandalized.

And loud.

Why was everything so loud this morning?

Since she was only restating the obvious, he ignored the question. "Your brother's right," he said to Jill as he filled his mug. "If you don't get a move on, you're going to miss the bus."

"And you can't give me a ride today, because you got drunk last night and left your truck in town."

He wasn't in the mood for her attitude today, but he managed to bite back the sharp retort that sprang to his lips, because his kids had been through a lot lately— even before they woke up to an empty driveway and immediately jumped to the conclusion that their father had bailed on them, too.

"One more thing before you go," he said, as his daughter started to flounce out of the room.

Jill turned back to face him, her expression defiant.

"Whether you like it or not, you're stuck with me," he said. "Because you and your brothers are the most important things in the world to me and I'm *never* going to leave you."

"We're *people* not *things*," she said indignantly.

But he saw the relief in her eyes before she turned away again.

He lifted his mug to his lips.

"I've got band practice after school today," Nicky said, when his sister had gone.

"I remember," Billy assured him.

"But I can skip it, since you don't have a vehicle to pick me up."

"I'll have my truck back before then," he promised, unwilling to let his middle child sacrifice the one thing he'd continued to show an interest in since his parents' separation. "You are not skipping band practice."

Nicky shrugged, as if it didn't matter. "Okay."

But it mattered to Billy, who'd promised himself that he would ensure his kids' lives were unaffected—as much as possible—by the divorce.

He swallowed another mouthful of coffee before shifting his attention to his eldest child. "What do you have going on today?"

"Nothin'," Branson said.

"I thought you mentioned something about a math test."

"Yeah."

"Did you study?"

"Yeah."

His firstborn had never been much of a talker, but

he'd shut down even more in recent months and his one-word responses had become the norm.

"Your aunt Stacy told me that there's a career fair at the high school this weekend," he said, in an effort to initiate an actual conversation. "Are you planning on going?"

"No way."

Well, at least that was two words.

"Why not?"

"Because it'll be the same as last year and the year before that."

And now a whole sentence—if only to express disinterest.

"She thought your sister might find it interesting."

Branson snorted. "Doubt it."

"I'm going to take her anyway," Billy decided. "You and Nicky should come, too."

"No, thanks."

"Just to clarify—that wasn't a request."

His eldest rolled his eyes.

"I've got band practice Saturday," Nicky said.

"Lucky you," Branson muttered.

"Too bad you don't have other plans," Billy said mildly.

"Maybe I do."

"Then I'd like to hear about them—and hanging out with your friends doesn't count."

"Does the Christmas food drive count?"

"Is that this weekend already?"

"It's always the weekend after the tree lighting," Nicky pointed out.

Which they'd skipped this year, because none of them had been feeling particularly festive.

But whether he was in the mood or not, apparently Christmas was just around the corner.

"Are you signed up to volunteer for the food drive?" he asked Branson now.

"I'll sign up today," he promised.

Billy could hardly object to his son doing volunteer work—even if his sole purpose in doing so was to avoid the career fair.

Or even to avoid spending time with his father.

He nodded and lifted his mug again, wincing when he realized his coffee had already gone cold.

Charlotte and Eloise had stayed up late into the night talking. Though they'd grown up in the same house—at least until Charlotte ran away—the seven-year gap in their ages had prevented them from being close when they were younger. So it was a pleasure to be able to reconnect with her sister now that they were both adults and discover that she genuinely liked the woman Eloise had become.

She was also a little bit in awe of everything that Eloise had accomplished—without any help from their family. And perhaps a little envious, too, that her sister had been able to live her life on her own terms—and choose to come home the same way. Because Bronco was obviously home to Eloise, despite the fact that she'd lived in New York for the past several years.

Of course, Charlotte had been gone a lot longer, and after two decades, she was less certain that Bronco was still her home. Truthfully, she wasn't sure she had a home. What she had, instead, was a tiny apartment south of Miami where she slept between research trips and educational tours.

For the past seven years, her work had been focused in and around the Bahamas, studying how resident marine mammals were impacted by increased commercial shipping in the area. But funding was often a challenge and she had some time off now while she waited for another research grant to come through, which was why she'd decided to pass the holidays in Bronco with her family.

She was looking forward to spending some time with Daniel, Seth and Ryan, her brothers who lived on the Triple T and worked at Taylor Beef, and with her sister Allison, whenever she made it home. But for now, Charlotte was happy to hang out with Eloise and Merry.

"What are you doing up already?" Eloise asked, when she came out of the bedroom in her robe and found the sofabed had been converted back to a sofa and her sister was already dressed.

"I'm revising a presentation."

"I thought you were on holidays."

"I am. But I ran into Michelle Lovett—my high school guidance counselor—at Bronco Java and Juice yesterday, and she asked if I'd be willing to participate in the career fair this Saturday."

"Your high school guidance counselor is still at the high school? Is she a hundred years old now?"

"Ha ha. She was actually really young back then."

"So…only ninety years old now."

Charlotte rolled her eyes.

"Okay, serious question," Eloise said. "Did it cross your mind—for even half a second—that you could say *no*?"

"Sure," she said. "But I think it'll be fun."

At least, that's what she was telling herself, though she was admittedly a little apprehensive about returning to the school she'd attended two decades earlier—the school where she'd fallen head over heels in love with Billy Abernathy. Because she knew the building would be filled with memories of times spent there with him. Memories that she'd probably avoided for far too long and that she'd continue to avoid if she could. But since Eloise had mentioned Billy's divorce the night before, that task was proving increasingly difficult.

"I think you've spent too much time in the ocean and your waterlogged brain has no concept of how rotten high school kids can be," Eloise remarked, drawing her sister's attention back to the present.

"I have spent a lot of time in the water," Charlotte admitted. "But I've also spent a lot of time educating people—including kids and teens—about the oceans and marine life and conservation, and I'm happy to have the opportunity to share some of the knowledge I've picked up over the years." She finished editing the slideshow she'd put together and closed the lid of her laptop. "Although today, the only thing I want to do is spend time with you and Merry."

"I'm glad," Eloise said. "Because that's what's on our agenda, too."

Chapter Three

"I can't believe you're making me go to school on a Saturday," Jill grumbled, when her father informed her of their plans for the day.

"At least it's not your school," Billy pointed out.

"I'm thirteen, Dad. Girls my age are supposed to be hanging out with their friends and talking about cute boys."

"If you're trying to convince me to let you hang out with your friends instead of going to the career fair, that was the wrong argument to make," he told her.

"My point is, I shouldn't have to be thinking about what I want to do with the rest of my life when I'm barely a teenager."

"It's never too early to plan for your future."

"So why aren't Branson and Nicky going?"

"Because they both went last year. Plus Branson is

volunteering for the food drive today and Nicky has band practice."

She sighed. "This was Aunt Stacy's idea, wasn't it?"

"Why would you say that?"

"Because I bet you wouldn't even have known the career fair was today if she hadn't told you."

"You've got me there," he admitted. Though his sister taught at Bronco Valley Elementary, she kept herself apprised of important events at both schools.

"Please don't make me go," Jill said now.

"This isn't up for discussion," he told her, determined to be firm. But damn, it was hard to refuse his little girl anything when she looked at him with pleading eyes.

She pouted—a slight protrusion of her lower lip.

Then her brow furrowed and she pressed a hand against her abdomen. "But I'm really not feeling well, Daddy. My stomach is tight and crampy. I think… I might be getting…my period."

"Nice try, Jilly Bean," he said. "I might actually have bought that one, if I hadn't had to stop at the store to get tampons for you last week."

The furrow turned into an outright scowl. "I bet Mom wouldn't make me go."

"I'd tell you to go ask her, but she doesn't live here anymore so she doesn't get a say."

"Well, maybe I should go live with her."

The deliberate blow hit its mark—and boomeranged back at her. Because they both knew that Jane hadn't invited her kids to live with her. The initial separation agreement had included a schedule for regular and holiday visitation, but Jane hadn't asked for custody. Not even joint custody.

And while he would be forever grateful that he hadn't had to do battle in order for Branson, Nicky and Jill to stay at the Bonnie B with him, he was also a little sad that Jane hadn't wanted to fight for them. And angry with her, too, because what kind of message did her indifference send to their kids? One that said they were only wanted for Wednesday-night dinners and every-other-weekend visits.

She'd claimed that she wanted to give them the stability of staying in their own home, because she knew they wouldn't be happy anywhere but at the Bonnie B, and maybe that was true. Or maybe it was just a convenient justification for her actions.

"We're leaving in thirty minutes," Billy warned his daughter now. "So unless you want to go to the career fair in your pajamas, I suggest you go get dressed."

"Can I at least call Alyssa and invite her to come with us?"

"Fine," he relented. "You can invite your friend."

Jill stomped down the stairs twenty-eight minutes later. She'd swapped the flannel pj's decorated with cartoon sheep for a plain white T-shirt tucked into high-waisted skinny jeans with a knit cardigan sweater that looked three sizes too big. Still, he was so happy she wasn't wearing the ripped jeans that exposed more of her thighs than they covered that he kept his mouth shut about the sweater. After all, what did he know about teenage fashion?

"Are we picking up Alyssa on the way?" he asked.

"No." Jill's tone was flat. "She has other plans."

"Did you want to ask one of your other friends? Kelli? Or Sam?"

"They're busy, too."

Apparently she hadn't spent the whole twenty-eight minutes getting dressed but trying to find someone—anyone—to go with her to make this dreaded career fair more bearable.

She moved past him to get her coat.

"Are you wearing mascara? And lipstick?"

"It's lip *gloss*," she told him.

"What have I told you about makeup?"

"That I can wear it when I go to high school. And today, you're making me go to high school."

He inclined his head. "Well played."

She smiled. "Thank you."

He called for Branson—who was brushing his teeth—to hurry up. Nicky had been waiting at the front door for ten minutes already. Finally, they all piled into his dual cab for the trip into town.

He dropped Nicky off at the back entrance, near the auditorium, and Branson hopped out with his brother, then Billy made his way to the main parking lot.

He walked through the front doors behind his daughter, watching as she signed in at the registration desk and wrote her name on an adhesive tag that she then slapped on her sweater. Billy let her venture ahead, respecting her request that he not hover, taking some time to peruse the displays as he walked by, offering a wave to a familiar face here and there and stopping once or twice to exchange a few words with someone he knew.

Wandering around his old high school on his own was a strange experience. He had mostly fond memories of the years he'd spent here—even if Charlotte Taylor played a starring role in most of those memories. They'd been friends since kindergarten, had shared their first real kiss in tenth grade (behind the equipment storage shed after a football game that their Mustangs lost to the Wolves from Wonderstone Ridge) and gone on their first official date three weeks later (a movie—*School of Rock*—at Bronco's recently opened multiplex). After that, they'd been pretty much inseparable, and no one was shocked when word started to spread, near the end of their senior year, that they were planning to get married.

Some of their friends might have been surprised to learn that the wedding was scheduled for the weekend immediately following high school graduation, but no one had ever doubted that Billy and Charlotte would exchange vows and eventually raise a family together on the Bonnie B.

Suffice it to say, Billy wasn't the only one who was surprised when his bride-to-be was a no-show at the altar.

But why was he thinking about her now?

Maybe it was passing the cafeteria where they'd eaten countless lunches together. Or walking through the halls that they'd often walked hand in hand. Or seeing the music practice room where they'd sometimes gone to make out when Mrs. Roy was teaching next door.

Or maybe it was his recent divorce—proof that he'd failed at yet another relationship—that made him think of his long-ago girlfriend and the wedding-that-never-happened.

Perhaps he should have taken Charlotte's abandonment as a sign and given up on the whole concept of happily ever after—or at least lifelong commitment. Of course he wished things had worked out differently with Jane, but even if he could go back in time knowing what the future held, he would still choose to marry her and have a family with her. Because he could go on without Jane, but he couldn't—didn't want to—imagine his life without Branson, Nicky and Jill.

Which was when he realized that his daughter was nowhere in sight.

Dammit.

He didn't let himself panic, because he didn't really think she'd disappeared. But he was annoyed—mostly with himself—that he'd lost sight of her.

The career fair was pretty crowded. Some jobs were obviously more interesting (at least in the eyes of the students) than others, as evidenced by the numbers crowded around certain tables and their lack at others. At the end of the aisle, Billy stepped aside and pulled his cell phone out of his pocket to send a quick message to Jill, trying hard not to let his anxiety get the better of him.

where r u?

Three little dots appeared on his screen—an indication that she was replying—and the knots of tension in his belly started to loosen.

science area

He tucked his phone back in his pocket and glanced around, looking toward the back of the gym and wishing that Jill had been a little more specific regarding her location.

"Can I help you find something, Billy?"

He glanced up to see Mrs. Lovett—his high school guidance counselor from way back. Of course he'd immediately recognized her, but he was a little surprised, considering the number of students who'd attended the school in the past twenty years, that she'd remembered his name.

"I'm looking for the science area."

"Back corner, near the boys' locker room."

"Thanks."

"Are you here with Branson or Nicky or both?" she asked him.

"Neither," he said. "Branson's helping out with the food drive and Nicky's practicing with the band. It's their sister, Jill—she'll be starting high school next September—who's here to check out potential career options."

"Getting a head start," Mrs. Lovett said approvingly. "Good for her."

He nodded. "Well, thanks for your help."

"That's why I'm here," she told him. "It was good to see you, Billy."

"You, too, Mrs. Lovett."

As he made his way toward the back of the gym, he wondered if there was anything in particular that had caught his daughter's attention or if she was just making her way through the displays.

Her report card grades consistently showed an aptitude for both science and math, which her teachers promised would open a lot of doors for her future education. Still, he couldn't help but think that if she was actually showing an interest in something, it would be a Christmas miracle.

As he approached the area, he breathed a quiet sigh of relief when he saw Jill in conversation with someone. She wasn't just talking but appeared genuinely engaged. She was even smiling instead of scowling for a change.

And her smile actually widened when she saw him approach.

"Here's my dad now," she said.

Billy stepped forward, eager to meet the person responsible for his daughter's animated demeanor—and found himself face-to-face with the one woman he was certain he never wanted to see again.

Charlotte was glad that Jill was still talking, because she wasn't sure that she would have been able to form a single word when she saw Billy Abernathy standing in front of her. His unexpected presence seemed to have caused a complete disconnect between the synapses of her brain and her mouth, and she was suddenly aware that she was standing face-to-face with the man she'd once loved with every fiber of her being.

The man she'd never forgotten.

Her first thought was that he looked good.

Even better than she remembered.

Of course, he'd been more of a boy than a man when she walked away from him twenty years earlier, and the cowboy standing in front of her now was every inch a man.

He stood a solid six feet, she guessed, emphasis on solid. His formerly lean build had certainly filled out. His shoulders were broader, his chest wider, his arms thicker. His stubble-covered jaw was square, with just the hint of a dent in his chin. His blond hair was a little darker and threaded with a few strands of gray. But his green eyes were the deep, rich color of moss that she remembered. And Charlotte belatedly realized why the girl she'd been talking to looked a little bit familiar to her—because Jill had the same eyes as the man who was obviously her father, right down to the ridiculously long lashes.

He was dressed like many of the other dads she'd seen wander through, in the typical rancher uniform of blue jeans, flannel shirt, cowboy boots and leather jacket. The difference was that her womanly parts hadn't tingled for any of the other men who'd walked past—but they were definitely tingling now.

Obviously she'd spent far too much time at sea in recent months.

"Miss Taylor has traveled all over the world studying dolphins," Jill said to her dad. "Where they live and what they eat. I thought she studied dolphins and whales, because there are lots of slides of killer whales, but killer whales aren't really whales at all—they're actually part of the dolphin family. Did you know that, Dad?"

"I did not." He was obviously responding to his daughter's question, but Billy's gaze was locked on Charlotte.

And while there had been a time when she could easily read his face to know what he was thinking and feeling, his expression was unreadable to her now.

"It's a common misconception," Charlotte said, managing to find her voice at last and join the conversation.

"Look at that." Jill nudged her dad and pointed to the picture on the laptop screen—a trio of dolphins swimming in turquoise waters shimmering gold in the sunset. "Isn't that the coolest thing ever?"

"It's a great picture," he agreed.

"That's in—" The girl looked at Charlotte for help. "I can't remember where you said that picture was taken."

"Bimini," she supplied.

"That's in the Bahamas," Jill added, for her father's benefit.

"I can't imagine there are many dolphins to study in Bronco, Montana," Billy remarked in a dry tone.

"You'd be right about that," Charlotte confirmed.

"So what brings a marine biologist to this landlocked part of the world?"

"I'm visiting my sister. Eloise just had a baby. A girl."

"I did hear something about that," he said. "Please pass along my congratulations.,"

"And since it's so close to Christmas, I thought I'd stick around," Charlotte continued. "It's been a long time since I celebrated the holidays with my family."

"I'm sure your parents are happy to have you home."

"I hope so," she said. It was hard to tell with her father. Thaddeus had squeezed her so tight she'd thought he might crack her ribs, but even before he'd released her from his embrace, he'd been grumbling about the work that would take her away again. Imogen had quickly blinked away her tears and immediately started making plans for all the things they could do together in preparation of the big day.

"Anyway, I was surprised to learn that Jill's still in middle school," she continued. "It's impressive to see someone so young thinking about a future career."

"It's never too soon to plan for the future," Jill quipped.

Billy slanted a look at his daughter.

"Wise words," he said dryly.

"Well, it so happens that I'm going to be speaking to some of the classes here next week in more detail about my work. And I thought, if Jill is really interested in marine biology, she might want to attend."

"I do," his daughter said excitedly. "I really do."

"Jill's got her own classes to attend next week," Billy said.

"Of course," Charlotte said, nodding. "Though I can't imagine her teacher would object to excusing her from class to attend a special presentation at the high school."

"Well, *I* object," he said. "I don't think she's ready to be plunked into the middle of class full of high schoolers."

"I'm going to be a student here next year," Jill reminded him.

Charlotte forced herself to remain silent, recognizing that this was an issue dad and daughter needed to work out between them.

"This was your idea," Jill said to her father now. "You wanted me to find something that interests me, and this does."

She had him there, Billy acknowledged, if only to himself.

And while he didn't want to extinguish the spark of interest, he had some concerns. Such as the obvious lack of job prospects for a marine biologist in Montana. And that his daughter seemed to want to follow in the footsteps of the woman—*first woman*, he amended—who'd run away from him.

The woman who, even now, caused an unwelcome stirring in his blood.

It had been twenty years, *dammit*.

This should *not* be happening.

But looking at Charlotte, the years seemed to melt away.

She certainly didn't look twenty years older.

In fact, she looked every bit as beautiful as she'd been at seventeen, with the same blonde hair (perhaps bleached a little lighter as a result of the hours she spent in the sun) and big blue eyes (with just a few fine lines at the corners), the same delicate nose (now with a sprinkling of freckles) and sweetly curved lips (that, even without any gloss or color, tempted a man to taste.)

Oh yeah, his blood was stirring.

And he was *not* happy about it.

"What day and time?" he finally asked Charlotte.

She consulted the calendar app on her phone. "I'll be here on Tuesday at 1:45 and Thursday at 12:30."

"We've only got half a day on Tuesday," Jill reminded him.

The fact that his daughter was willing to give up a

free afternoon convinced him that she wasn't feigning her interest.

Which meant that he was going to have to grit his teeth and accede to her request.

"Then I guess we'll see you Tuesday at 1:45," he said to Charlotte.

And Jill smiled. At him.

Her smiles were so rare these days, he would do almost anything to get one—even sit in a classroom for a science lecture given by his runaway bride.

Chapter Four

Charlotte hadn't been particularly busy during the career fair, and she wasn't surprised. Though Bronco had grown a lot in the past twenty years—and continued to grow—cattle remained the area's primary industry and she'd suspected that even if her research focus had been on sea cows, most of the students would have walked on by.

So it was ironic that one of the few students with whom she'd exchanged more than a handful of words had turned out to be her former fiancé's teenage daughter.

She'd known, of course, that Billy had a family. Just because she hadn't spent a lot of time in Bronco over the past two decades didn't mean that she hadn't been kept apprised of the town's happenings by various family members. She'd been informed of his marriage (probably within hours of the vows being exchanged!) and the birth of his first child—a son—followed two years later by another son and two years after that by a daughter.

But knowing that he had three kids was a lot different than finding herself face-to-face with one of those kids.

Jill Abernathy wasn't just a beautiful girl, she was also intelligent and articulate. She'd been drawn by the photos of the dolphins—which was exactly why Charlotte included them in her presentation materials—but she'd asked smart questions about the mammals and their habitat.

Charlotte had sincerely enjoyed talking to Jill—until the realization that she was Billy's daughter had landed like a sucker punch to the gut.

So maybe she shouldn't have invited her to come back to the school, increasing the likelihood that she would cross paths with Billy again. But she couldn't let her personal feelings get in the way of doing her job. Part of that job was education, and if, in the process, she managed to interest more people in the important work of marine conservation, all the better.

Not long after Billy and his daughter walked away, the career fair ended and Charlotte packed up her presentation materials. The teachers who'd been in attendance at the event all seemed to think it had gone well, and Vanessa John had made a point of stopping by Charlotte's table to reconfirm that she was available to speak to the science classes on Tuesday and Thursday.

Charlotte assured her that she was and also let her know that she'd invited a guest who'd seemed keen on learning more about marine biology to attend the Tuesday presentation. Vanessa had no objections—in fact, she said she was eager to meet Jill Abernathy, as she'd taught Jill's brother, Nicky, the previous year.

Because to Vanessa John, Jill was Nicky Abernathy's little sister. But to Charlotte, the girl was Billy's daughter.

And Charlotte's heart pinched again, thinking of the child they'd lost so many years earlier.

At the time, she'd been certain—despite the loss—that she'd be a mother someday. But it was hard to maintain a relationship when she was gone for months at a time, and getting involved with someone she worked in close quarters with for extended periods was inherently fraught with complications. A lesson she'd learned the hard way.

But somehow, suddenly, she was thirty-seven years old and the certainty that motherhood was somewhere in her future was slipping away.

She pushed the melancholy aside as she headed back to her sister's hotel, stopping on the way to pick up pizza from Bronco Brick Oven.

She was enjoying spending time with her sister and niece, and was pleased to discover that she liked Dante, too. He was handsome and charming and, most important, he was obviously head over heels in love with Eloise. She was glad that her sister had found such a great guy—especially after being abandoned by her ex as soon as he learned of her pregnancy—and happy to see Dante dote on Merry as if she were his own child.

"So how was the career fair?" Dante asked, when the pizza box was almost empty.

"The teachers seemed pleased with the turnout of students," Charlotte said.

"Did you happen to cross paths with any of your teachers—or classmates—from way back when?" Eloise wanted to know.

"Well, Michelle Lovett, obviously, as she's the one who asked me to participate," she replied. "And Mr. Kerry, my tenth grade history teacher. I also saw Leanne Rykell and Lori Dittmar and—" she peeled a slice of pepperoni off her pizza and popped it in her mouth "—Billy Abernathy."

"Ohmygod." Her sister practically squealed with excitement. "You have to tell me everything."

Dante glanced from one sister to the other. "I'm obviously missing something."

"A very big something," Eloise said. "Billy Abernathy was my sister's high school sweetheart."

"Is he the one you were engaged to when you did your runaway bride thing?"

Charlotte looked at her sister, an eyebrow raised.

Eloise shook her head. "I didn't tell him."

"Was it supposed to be a secret?" he asked.

"No," Charlotte said.

"But now I want to know how you know," Eloise said.

Dante wiped his fingers on a paper napkin. "In the lunchroom yesterday, I mentioned that Charlotte was in town and Stacy Abernathy referred to her as Bronco's own runaway bride—though she failed to mention that her brother was the intended groom."

"Julia Roberts ran out on four weddings—I only ran out on one," Charlotte said, a little defensively.

"But she did run," Eloise noted. "Literally kicked off her shoes and hightailed it out of there."

"How do *you* know that?" Charlotte asked.

"Dad was standing with me and Allison—we were junior bridesmaids," Eloise explained to Dante. "Anyway, we were by the windows in the vestibule, waiting for you to come inside so the wedding could start, and we saw you take off." She smirked at the memory. "I have never heard Daddy swear like he swore that day. And in church even."

"Glad to know I'm a source of entertainment for the community still," Charlotte remarked dryly.

"It was a pretty big scandal at the time," her sister said. "But I don't think people are talking about it still."

"Except in the lunchroom at Bronco Valley Elementary School."

Eloise cocked her head, as if listening for something. "I think I hear Merry stirring."

Charlotte didn't hear any such thing—and the video feed from the baby monitor, displayed on the tablet propped up on the table, showed the baby to be sleeping soundly.

But apparently Dante could take a hint, because he pushed away from the table and said, "I'll go check on her."

"I don't know why you sent him away," Charlotte said to her sister when he was gone. "All my secrets are out in the open."

"I didn't know if you'd want to talk about Billy in front of Dante."

"I don't want to talk about Billy at all—because there's nothing to talk about."

"Well, I want to talk about him," Eloise said. "I want you to recount every word that was spoken and tell me about every glance that was exchanged."

"There really isn't much to tell. We talked about my research. His daughter seems interested in marine biology, so I invited her to come to one of the lectures I'm giving next week."

"Did you ask him how he was?" Eloise pressed, clearly not satisfied with her sister's answer. "Did you tell him he looked good? Did he look good?"

"No," Charlotte said. "We didn't talk about anything personal. Actually, that's not entirely true—I told him that I was in town visiting you and your new baby, and he said to pass along his congratulations."

"You didn't answer my last question," Eloise noted.

"What was your last question?"

"Did he look good?"

"He looked…" Strong. Solid. Sexy. "Like Billy."

"Uh-huh." Her sister's smile was knowing. "And the way Billy looks makes you hot. Don't even try to deny it," she said, when Charlotte opened her mouth to respond. "Because your cheeks are flushed."

"Maybe it's warm in here," she said.

"Not *that* warm," Eloise said.

Charlotte sighed.

But if she couldn't talk to her sister, who could she talk to?

"Okay, yes. He looked really good. And maybe I didn't expect to think so. I mean, it's been twenty years. Shouldn't I be…immune or something?"

"First love can be a powerful thing," Eloise noted.

"Apparently." She sighed again.

"Was there any kind of spark?" her sister asked hopefully.

"Maybe a spark of anger on his part," Charlotte allowed. "He did *not* seem particularly happy to see me chatting with his daughter."

"I'm sure he was surprised. I know you've been back to visit family over the years, but you haven't crossed paths with him before now, have you?"

"No."

"Are you going to see him again?"

"Possibly Tuesday, if he brings Jill to Vanessa John's class for my presentation. But I wouldn't be surprised if he just dropped her off and told her to take the bus home so that he doesn't have to cross paths with me again."

"Wear something pretty, just in case."

"I'm not sure I brought anything that would qualify as pretty," Charlotte said. "Or anything that qualifies as warm. I've spent so much time in the Bahamas over the past few years, it seems I forgot how cold Montana is in December."

"You can raid my closet," Eloise told her. "Or—here's an even better idea—we could go shopping."

"I do need to do some shopping," she agreed. "But for Christmas gifts. I don't want to waste time—or money—on clothes I'll only wear for a couple of weeks."

"Speaking of Christmas shopping…" Eloise said.

"Anytime."

Her sister smiled at Charlotte's enthusiastic response, not guessing that she was mostly eager to change the subject to something other than Billy Abernathy.

"Actually, I was going to ask if there was any chance you'd be willing to babysit one night so that Dante and I could do some shopping."

"Are you kidding? That's an even better plan."

"I'll admit, I'm still a little uncertain about leaving her. I don't mean with you," Eloise hastened to assure her sister. "I just mean at all. She's still so tiny and I'm not thrilled with the idea of taking her to crowded shops where she's likely to be cooed over by well-meaning but potentially germ-carrying strangers."

"I understand your concerns," Charlotte said. "And I promise to make myself available whenever you want, if you decide you want to venture out."

"Thanks."

"My pleasure," she said, knowing that she was the one who should be thanking her sister—because Charlotte felt confident that her adorable niece was the one person who could keep her mind off thoughts of Billy Abernathy.

Billy was programming the temperature to preheat the oven when Nicky wandered into the kitchen.

"What's for supper?" he asked.

"Chicken pot pie."

His son made a face. "Didn't we have chicken pot pie last week?"

"Yep." But he'd wanted something easy—something

he didn't have to think about—because his mind had been reeling since his encounter with Charlotte at the career fair.

He should have known it was inevitable that their paths would cross someday. She might have left Bronco twenty years ago, but most of her family still lived here, which meant that she occasionally returned to town to see them.

But two decades without any contact had apparently lulled him into a false sense of security. And then, out of the blue, she was there, and he suddenly realized how completely ill-prepared he was to see her again and feel all the things that being near her made him feel.

Loss. Grief. Regret.

Of course, those were only the tip of the iceberg, and he wasn't at all eager to find out what murkier emotions might exist beneath the surface.

"Can't we have something else tonight? Like pizza?" Nicky asked hopefully, oblivious to his dad's preoccupation.

Billy forced his attention back to the subject of dinner. "We had pizza last week, too," he pointed out.

"Yeah, but pizza's good."

"Are you saying you don't like your grandmother's chicken pot pie?"

"It's not my favorite," Nicky said.

"Then you should tell her that, because we have three more in the freezer."

His son sighed. "Maybe we could have the pie tomorrow night, when everyone will be home to enjoy it?"

"You mean when Branson's home to eat his share?" Billy guessed.

Before Nicky could respond to that, Jill walked into the room and asked, "What's for supper?"

"Chicken pot pie," Nicky told her.

Jill made a face eerily similar to the one Billy had seen on her brother not two minutes earlier.

"It's not fair that Branson gets to go out with his friends and we have to have chicken pot pie," she protested.

"Here's a news flash," Billy said. "Life's not fair."

"Yeah, because our mom moving out to live with her French teacher didn't teach us that lesson already," she retorted.

The reminder that his kids had already gotten a raw deal tipped the scales—or maybe he just wasn't up to battling over something as inconsequential as the dinner menu.

"Okay, we'll save the pie for tomorrow night," he decided, turning off the oven. "Grab your coats—we'll go into town for pizza."

For once, his kids didn't need to be told twice.

But if pizza had seemed like a good idea at the time they were leaving the ranch, when they arrived at Bronco Brick Oven Pizza, he discovered that it was also a very popular idea.

While they were waiting for a table, he scanned the interior of the restaurant. His heart skipped a beat when he saw a blond woman seated in a corner booth, her hair in a familiar ponytail, and silently cursed himself for agreeing to his kids' request for pizza.

Then the woman turned her head to speak to her companion, giving him a view of her profile.

Not Charlotte.

Even as he breathed a quiet sigh of relief, he realized that he was just a little bit disappointed—and how messed up was that?

Thirty minutes later, Billy, Nicky and Jill were finally seated. As they'd already had time to thoroughly peruse the menu, they ordered right away.

They were sipping their drinks and waiting for their pizza when he caught a glimpse of another woman who looked familiar.

Unfortunately, this time his identification was not mistaken.

It was his ex-wife—and her new lover.

Merde.

See? He could speak French, too (even if that particular word was only one of half a dozen that he knew from reading subtitles in movies) and he didn't need to sleep with a French teacher to learn it.

"Hey, look." Jill started waving her arm in the air to get her mother's attention. "Mom's here."

"Not just Mom," Nicky muttered.

Jill immediately dropped her arm.

But it was too late. Jane and Henri had spotted Jill—and Nicky and Billy—and came over to say "hi."

"Busy place tonight," Henri remarked.

"It's always busy on Saturday nights," Nicky said, repeating what his father told him when they'd had to wait thirty minutes for a table.

"Where's Branson?" Jane asked.

"Out with friends."

"In that case, it looks like you've got enough room for us to join you."

He sent her a look that he had no doubt spoke the volumes he didn't dare say aloud because he was trying to keep things civil with his ex—at least in front of the kids.

"We've already put our names on the list," Henri reminded her.

"And were told there's nearly an hour wait," Jane replied.

Nicky glanced at his dad, obviously waiting to take his cue from him. Billy looked at Jill.

"Do you guys want to squeeze in?" he asked, leaving the choice up to his kids.

Nicky offered a shrug; Jill gave a tentative nod.

"Please, join us," Billy invited, speaking through clenched teeth.

Jane immediately sat on the edge of the bench beside Nicky, leaving Henri to take the seat across from her—beside Billy.

As Billy herded Nicky and Jill out to his truck at the conclusion of a painfully awkward meal, he figured it would be a long time before either of them grumbled about chicken pot pie again.

But he hadn't even pulled out of the parking lot when Nicky started grumbling on a different topic.

"I can't believe you waved at them," he sniped at his sister. "What were you thinking?"

"I didn't wave at *them*," Jill protested. "I waved at *Mom*."

"When is Mom ever not with *him*?" Nicky demanded.

"I...forgot," she said.

"It's bad enough we have to have dinner with them every Wednesday, but you had to go ahead and ruin a perfectly good Saturday!"

"I'm sorry!" she shouted back, tears glistening in her eyes.

"The night wasn't ruined," Billy felt compelled to interject.

"Were you sitting at the same table?" Nicky's tone dripped with disbelief.

"Well, the pizza was good," he said. "And Henri picked up the check."

"He can afford it," Nicky said.

"Why would you say that?" Billy asked. As far as he knew, teachers—especially those who only worked part-time—weren't particularly well paid.

"His parents own some big winery and a fancy house in France."

"A chalet," Jill chimed in, proving that she'd paid more attention to the details than her brother. "In Bordeaux."

"They're planning to visit there in the summer," Nicky said.

"And they want to take us with them."

"First I've heard," Billy muttered.

"I don't wanna go," Nicky assured him.

Jill didn't say anything.

Because she wanted to visit Henri's parents' fancy house in Bordeaux? Or because she wanted to spend more time with her mother?

Billy suspected the reason for her silence was likely the latter, and he didn't blame her. While he'd made it clear to his kids that there were no sides to be taken—that sometimes marriages didn't work out and it wasn't necessarily the fault of one party or the other—the boys had clearly interpreted Jane's decision to leave the family home as evidence that she'd been the one to pull the plug on their marriage. Jill was just as unhappy as her brothers about the splitting up of their family, but she was a thirteen-year-old girl who, understandably, craved the attention of her mother.

And if she wanted to spend a couple of weeks—or even the whole summer—in France with Jane and Henri, Billy was going to have to suck it up and let her.

He only hoped he could do so without letting his daughter see how much he wouldn't like it.

Chapter Five

"Don't forget to pick me up at lunch for the marine biology presentation at the high school," Jill said to her dad, as she was stuffing books into her backpack Tuesday morning.

Billy only wished he could forget, but his daughter's frequent reminders about the event made it impossible for him to do so.

"I'll be there at twelve on the dot," he promised.

"Which is actually lunchtime," she pointed out.

"You don't say."

"And the lecture doesn't start until one forty-five, so we should have time to grab a quick bite somewhere first?" she asked hopefully.

"Or eat the lunch that is already packed in your lunch-box," he said.

"I don't usually take a lunch on half days, because I come home for lunch."

"Actually, that sounds like a better idea," he said. "I'll pick you up and we'll come home for lunch."

She rolled her eyes. "Why don't you want me to go to the presentation? Do you really think I'm too stupid to understand what's going on in a high school class?"

"Of course not," he immediately denied. "I just don't think you're ready for the high school environment." And he wasn't ready to see Charlotte Taylor again.

"I live with two brothers who are both in high school," she pointed out reasonably. "Somehow I doubt a classroom full of high schoolers is grosser than Branson and Nicky's bathroom."

He had to smile at that.

The truth was, he didn't object to Jill going so much as he objected to having to take her. Not only because it would cut into the middle of his day, but also—and maybe especially—because Charlotte Taylor had been cutting into his thoughts far too frequently since he'd seen her at the career fair. And haunting his dreams every night.

Though he would have thought it was impossible, his high school sweetheart was even more gorgeous now than she'd been at seventeen. But instead of thinking about how fabulous she'd looked, he should be reminding his heart—the same one she'd once trampled all over with ivory satin stilettos—that it had no business beating a little faster just because she was near.

Especially since she'd been gone for more years than

he'd known her, which meant that he didn't know her
at all anymore.

But he wanted to.

He was curious to know what she'd been doing the
past two decades, and maybe this lecture was his chance
to find out how she got from Bronco, Montana to studying marine biology and what her job actually entailed.

"Dad?"

His daughter's impatient query jolted Billy back to
the present.

"What?"

"I have to go catch the bus." She brushed a quick kiss
on his cheek. "But I'll see you at noon."

"On the dot," he said again.

Even after stopping for lunch, they were early for
the class, which allowed Billy the opportunity to chat
for a minute with Vanessa John—who'd taught Nicky
the previous year. The teacher invited Jill to sit at the
front of the class, and Billy took a seat at the back, to
give her some space.

When Charlotte wandered in with a group of students, for a moment, Billy felt as if he was in tenth grade
again—and totally infatuated with the prettiest girl in
school. She spoke to Vanessa for a few minutes, then
got busy connecting cables to her laptop. Soon, the pull-
down screen at the front of the classroom displayed the
same "dolphins at sunset" photo that had captivated his
daughter at the career fair.

The students immediately settled and focused their
attention on Charlotte at the front of the class. She was

wearing almost the exact same uniform she'd worn on Saturday—a dark blue T-shirt with turquoise letters that spelled out Dolphin Harbour Project in the shape of a dolphin along with a pair of hip-hugging jeans and bright pink running shoes.

For the first thirty minutes of the class, she talked about a "Day in the Life of a Marine Biologist" then proceeded to explain why there was no such thing as an average day, which was only one of the reasons that her job was so much fun. Apparently her assignments might include research at sea or tests or studies in a lab or education in a classroom—like she was doing now.

When she opened up for questions, at least a dozen hands shot into the air. One student wanted to know all the places she'd worked, in response to which Charlotte rattled off the names of several islands, some of which Billy had never heard of.

Another student asked if she had a favorite kind of dolphin. She replied that she loved them all but admitted to a particular fondness for Atlantic spotted dolphins, which were the focus of her current research.

She talked about her work not just with authority but with passion, and he was pleased to know that she'd found a career she obviously enjoyed. Still, he couldn't help but wonder if she truly had everything she wanted.

When they'd been in high school, they'd shared their hopes and dreams for the future, and they'd both expressed hope of having a family someday. That *someday* had almost come a lot sooner than they'd imagined— until the baby she'd carried slipped away, leaving them with no evidence that it had ever existed. No evidence except for the scars on both their hearts.

He'd cried right along with her when she told him about the miscarriage. Both of them grieving; both of them secretly relieved. Because they were barely more than kids themselves—no way were they ready to have one. Still, even while they mourned their baby, they'd been confident they would have another child someday, after they were married.

But their wedding never happened. Instead, Billy had stood alone at the altar, grieving then for the loss of the girl he'd always loved.

The same girl—now a woman—who was holding Vanessa John's science class captivated with her tales of the big blue sea. And while he wouldn't have chosen to be there, he could appreciate that she was great with the kids, answering their questions in terms that they could understand and illustrating with appropriate anecdotes.

The next question was an interesting one—had she ever gotten seasick? She admitted that her research group had once been caught in the middle of an unexpected tropical storm and that they'd all been throwing up over the side of the boat.

This confession led to a follow-up question about sharks being attracted by vomit and other bodily fluids (not true, she said) and the revelation that it was unlikely there would have been any sharks around, anyway, as they, and other marine life, were so sensitive to barometric pressure drops—which indicate a storm is coming—they would swim out to deeper water where they'd be safer.

Three boys, sitting close together not far from Billy, whispered among themselves for a few minutes before one of the group finally lifted his hand.

"Have you ever seen dolphins having sex?" he asked, when Charlotte called on him.

Though she didn't seem at all fazed by the question, the teacher immediately jumped in to respond before her guest could do so.

"That's a good question, Reece," Ms. John said. "And if you're really interested in learning more, you're welcome to stay after class so that we can talk about it."

Reece slunk down in his seat.

His buddies snickered.

The teacher's gaze shifted to them. "Devon and Kurt can stay, too."

"What did we do?" Devon (or Kurt) demanded.

"We didn't do anything," Kurt (or Devon) protested.

"You dared him," Ms. John said, proving that she knew her students well.

They fell silent with almost identical sulky expressions on their faces.

"And that's all the time we've got," she said to the rest of the class.

Some of the students were already packing up their stuff, but others were clearly unhappy that the time was up.

"I don't want anyone to miss a bus or band practice or basketball game," Charlotte said. "But I'm happy to hang around a little longer to answer more questions."

Several students took that as their cue to approach for a more private conversation.

Billy joined the stream of kids making their way from the back of the room to the front, pausing by the desk at which his daughter was still seated.

"Let's go, Jilly Bean," he said.

"Can't we stay a little longer?"

"Class is over," he reminded her.

"But Miss Taylor is still answering questions."

"Do you have a question?" he asked.

"No," she admitted. "But I might be interested in hearing the answer to a question someone else asks."

"Your brothers are going to be waiting for us."

She huffed out a breath but tucked her notebook and pen (yes, he'd watched her taking copious notes while the marine biologist talked) into her backpack before zipping it up and slinging it over her shoulder.

As he steered her toward the door, Charlotte glanced over.

She lifted her hand to wave, and Jill happily waved back.

Then Charlotte's gaze locked with Billy's and she smiled.

He didn't smile back.

Charlotte loved talking about her job almost as much as she loved her job, and she was happy that a handful of students hung around to chat even after their teacher had dismissed the class. She was a little disappointed that Jill wasn't one of those students, but Billy had clearly been in a hurry to usher his daughter out of the classroom. So much in a hurry, apparently, that he couldn't even spare a fraction of a second to offer her a smile.

Of course, it was entirely possible that his grim demeanor was less about time constraints than it was his feelings toward Charlotte. And that would be a much bigger disappointment.

"Bronco must seem like a totally different world compared to all the other places you've been," Vanessa said, when the last of the students had gone and Charlotte was packing up her laptop.

"It is, indeed," she agreed. "Although it might be more appropriate to say that those places are a world away from here—which is where I grew up."

"Michelle didn't mention that you were from Bronco," Vanessa said, obviously surprised by this revelation. "Or maybe she assumed I'd figure it out, as the Taylor name is such an important one in this town."

"It's also a fairly common name," Charlotte acknowledged. "But yes, I am one of *those* Taylors. And not only did I go to school here, Michelle was my guidance counselor back then—which is why I always want to call her Mrs. Lovett rather than Michelle."

The teacher chuckled at that.

"If you were a student here," she said, as they exited the classroom together, "I'm wondering now if you knew Jill Abernathy's dad in high school."

"I did," she confirmed.

"I guess that would explain the look," Vanessa mused.

"What look?"

"The look he gave you as he walked out."

"Was there a look?"

"You know there was a look," the teacher chided.

Charlotte couldn't feign ignorance any longer. "Okay, but I don't know how to interpret it," she admitted.

"Then perhaps you should talk to him about it."

"Perhaps," she said.

Thankfully, Vanessa didn't pursue the topic any further.

Instead she thanked Charlotte for her time and said she was looking forward to seeing her on Thursday.

"I hope you won't be completely bored to hear the same presentation again."

"Are you kidding? I'm sincerely fascinated by what you do. And it's interesting to see what questions the kids come up with."

"Just so you know, whenever I talk to high schoolers, there's always someone who asks about sex," Charlotte said.

"Are you saying I shouldn't be too hard on the boys?"

"I wouldn't presume to tell you how to deal with your students," she assured the teacher. "I'm just saying it's something a lot of people wonder about—and I'm sure you know that boys that age are always thinking about sex, though probably not usually in relation to marine mammals."

To be fair, teenage girls spent a fair amount of time thinking about the subject, too. Certainly Charlotte had done so when she was in high school, and when she and Billy had decided to be intimate, it was because they'd both wanted to take their relationship to the next level.

Which wasn't something she should be thinking about now. Or ever.

But as she walked out of the classroom, she found herself wondering why he'd been in such a hurry. Did he have somewhere to be? Or was he afraid that he might get stuck having to make conversation with her again?

Had she hurt him so badly that, after more than twenty years, they couldn't exchange basic pleasantries when their paths crossed? Or was it the recent failure of his marriage that was responsible for his less than jovial mood?

Whatever the reason, she couldn't help but wonder if they'd ever have a chance to talk. Maybe it was two decades too late, but she wanted to explain why she'd made the difficult choice to walk out on their wedding.

But maybe he didn't want to hear her reasons. Maybe it really was ancient history. Water under the bridge and all kinds of other clichés that failed to explain why—after so much time had passed—she still got butterflies in her stomach when he was near.

Dammit, she was a grown woman. She should *not* be acting like a teenage girl in the presence of her first crush.

Even if Billy Abernathy had been exactly that—and so much more.

But she'd moved on. And so had he. She'd had other boyfriends and even a few lovers. He'd been married and had three kids. So it was crazy to think there could be any kind of spark between them still.

Or again.

It was her sister's fault, Charlotte decided. All of

Eloise's questions about Billy and her comments about their past had started her reminiscing, remembering all the happy times they'd shared and dreams for their future together.

Her reality had turned out very different, and most of the time she was happy with her life. But spending time with Eloise and Dante and Merry—seeing her sister as part of a family—had Charlotte feeling a little wistful.

So it was probably a good idea that she was staying at her parents' place for the next few days. A couple hours in the company of Thaddeus and Imogen would bring her back to reality.

"I should have made you all take the bus home," Billy groused, as Branson and Nicky's argument about who got to ride shotgun escalated into a shoving match in the parking lot. It seemed as if all his kids did lately was bicker and fight, and it was starting to grate on his nerves.

And weren't they a little old to be acting out because their parents had gotten divorced?

Of course, it was possible this wasn't new behavior— in which case, he had to wonder how Jane managed to keep all their lives running so effortlessly.

Or perhaps it hadn't been nearly as effortless as he'd wanted to believe. Because the truth was, he'd let his wife be responsible for the kids and their day-to-day activities while he focused on the ranch.

Maybe that was another reason that she'd been so eager to get out of the house once a week to go to French class.

Not that he was blaming his kids. Of course not. He knew that he was one hundred percent responsible for the failure of his marriage, because his wife had obviously been looking for something more than he could give her.

Apparently she'd found that *something* with Henri. And maybe one day Billy would find it in his heart to be happy for her, but today was not that day. Today he was still furious that she'd upended all of their lives to find her own bliss—whatever the hell that was supposed to mean.

"You guys have until the count of three to get in the truck and…" His intended threat to drive away without them trailed off when he spotted Charlotte making her way across the parking lot.

She lifted a hand to push back a strand of hair that blew across her face. Her left hand—bare of any rings on her fingers.

She didn't have any adornment on her right hand, either. He'd noticed that during her presentation. Not that he'd been looking or wondering—it was just that she was one of those people who used her hands when she talked, so it was hard not to notice.

He certainly didn't care about her marital status, though he was certain she'd never married, because he knew someone in Bronco would have told him if she had.

"Who's that?" Branson demanded.

"That's Miss Taylor," Jill said, in response to her brother's question. "The marine biologist who gave the presentation to Ms. John's science class."

"No kidding," Nicky mused. "Maybe I should check out her…presentation on Thursday."

"Gross," Branson said.

"She's not gross—she's hot," Nicky argued.

"It's gross that you think she's hot," Branson told him. "She's old."

"I don't think she's *that* old," Jill protested.

"Thirty-seven." Billy volunteered the information without thinking.

"That *is* old," Nicky agreed.

His siblings nodded their agreement.

"How do you know how old she is?" Jill asked curiously.

"We went to high school together," he admitted, aware that his response was only going to lead to more questions.

She frowned. "Why didn't you mention that when we saw her at the career fair on Saturday?"

He shrugged. "I didn't think it was important. It's not important."

But his daughter obviously had a different opinion—and an excuse now to approach Miss Taylor. Who, it turned out, was parked only a few spaces away from his vehicle.

"My dad just told me that you guys went to high school together," Jill said to Charlotte.

"That's true," she confirmed.

"So—what was he like back then?"

Charlotte's gaze shifted to him for a moment before she responded to his daughter's question. "He was… my best friend."

Billy couldn't disagree with the characterization, though *friends* was the least of what they'd been to one another way back then.

Jill wrinkled her nose. "Your best friend was a *boy*?"

Charlotte smiled as she glanced in his direction again. "And not just when we were in high school, but all through grade school, too."

"Wow. So you've known my dad for a *really* long time."

"Knew," she clarified. "We lost touch when I went away to college."

"How come?"

Now Charlotte shrugged. "Sometimes people just grow and change and move in different directions."

"Like my friend Meghan—she moved to Bozeman last summer," Jill said.

"Like that," his long-ago fiancée agreed. "Anyway, I'm glad you made it to the presentation today, but now I have to run. I'm supposed to be doing some Christmas baking with my mom tonight and I still have to stop by the grocery store to get the ingredients we need."

"Okay," Jill said, and Billy watched the happiness leak out of her like air out of a punctured balloon.

He knew it wasn't because Charlotte had brushed her off—it was the mention of baking with her mom, which was something Jill used to do with hers before Jane moved out, that was responsible for his daughter's abrupt mood change.

He drove the kids back to the ranch and waited for them to scatter before sending a text message to his ex.

A few minutes later, Jill came bouncing into the kitchen and began rummaging through the cupboards.

"Are you looking for anything in particular?" he asked.

"The box of cookie cutters."

He reached into the cupboard over the fridge to retrieve it for her.

"Thanks."

"What do you need it for?"

"Mom just called and asked me to bring it when we go for our visit this weekend, so that we can make cookies together."

"Did she?"

"I was just thinking that we probably weren't going to make them this year, and then she called. It was almost as if she could read my mind."

"Imagine that," he said.

Then her happy expression faded. "But what are you going to do this weekend?"

"Not bake cookies, now that you're taking the cutters."

"I'm serious, Dad. Are you going to be okay?"

"I'll be just fine, Jilly Bean. I promise."

She didn't look convinced.

"But if you're really worried—not that you should be, but if you are—there's something you could do for me," he said.

"What's that?"

"Promise to bring home some cookies."

Her smile returned. "I can do that."

"You made it." Imogen's greeting was filled with relief when she met Charlotte at the door to the family home on the Triple T.

"Did you think I'd get lost between the grocery store and here?"

"Of course not," her mother said, helping her with the shopping bags. "I just wasn't entirely sure you'd actually show up."

"Why wouldn't I? Holiday baking with you is one of my favorite Christmas traditions." Perhaps because it was the only time of year that her mom not only got her hands dirty in the kitchen but genuinely seemed to enjoy doing so.

Imogen busied herself unpacking the groceries. "You were out of here so quick after Thanksgiving, I almost thought you'd change your mind about coming back for Christmas."

"I might have," Charlotte admitted. "If I had anywhere else to go."

"Then I'm glad you didn't."

"I was kidding, Mom."

Imogen turned to look at her. "Were you?"

She shrugged. "Mostly."

Her mother sighed. "I just wish you and your sisters could be a little more…tolerant…when you're talking with your father."

"You think we should tolerate a man who's chauvinistic, opinionated and overbearing?"

"He's your father and he loves you, even if he doesn't know how to show it."

"I've been looking forward to baking with you all day," Charlotte said. "Can we please not ruin it by talking about Dad?"

"Fine," Imogen agreed. "What would you like to talk about?"

"Actually, I think instead of talking we should be singing."

Her mom smiled. "Google, play Christmas tunes."

And for the next four hours, Charlotte and her mom measured and mixed and baked, all the while singing and dancing to holiday classics. And when the last tray of cookies was taken out of the oven, Charlotte was in complete agreement with Perry Como—there was no place like home for the holidays.

Chapter Six

Since Charlotte had nothing on the schedule the following day, she decided to do some Christmas shopping at Holiday House. It had always been a favorite destination when she was a kid, and though it was under new ownership now as Sadie's Holiday House, Imogen had assured her that it was even better than she remembered.

The display in the huge front window apparently changed with the seasons and right now the display was themed to "The Twelve Days of Christmas," as noted by the elegantly painted words across the top of the window. Below the title were twelve wreaths—arranged in three rows of four—each one decorated to correspond with a verse of the famous song. Charlotte might have expected the "partridge in a pear tree" wreath to appear simple and boring in comparison to the one with "twelve drummers drumming," but whoever had created the pieces had taken care so that each was elaborately decorated without losing focus on the theme.

"Sadie does pretty fabulous work, doesn't she?"

The question startled her. Charlotte had been so caught up in her perusal of the window display that she hadn't heard him come up behind her—but she was even more startled by the fact that Billy had willingly approached her and initiated conversation.

Okay, maybe one question didn't necessarily lead to a conversation, but still, it gave her hope.

"You think she made the wreaths?" she asked, doing her part to keep the dialogue going.

"I know she did," he confirmed. "Her custom wreaths are very popular."

"I can see why," she noted.

She also noted that he was carrying a bag stamped with the store's logo.

"So what brings you into town two days in a row?"

"I had some errands that I didn't have a chance to complete yesterday because I was sitting in on a marine biology presentation," he said, proving that while he might have initiated this discussion, he obviously hadn't warmed up to her.

"I'm sorry if you feel your time was wasted."

"I didn't say that."

"You're right," she acknowledged. "But it seemed to be what you were implying."

"I wasn't implying anything," he denied. "I was just commenting that there aren't ever enough hours to do everything that needs to be done."

"Does that mean you don't have time to grab a cup of coffee?" she asked.

He hesitated, and she braced herself for rejection.

Why had she even made the overture?

It was obvious he wasn't entirely comfortable around her, so she was more than a little surprised when he glanced at the watch on his wrist then said, "Actually, a cup of coffee sounds good. But weren't you on your way into Sadie's Holiday House?"

"I can come back later," she decided.

They walked across the street to Bean & Biscotti, and though Charlotte tried to argue that she should be the one to pay because she'd invited him, he overruled her with a quicker draw of his bank card.

When they had their drinks—black coffee for each of them plus a warm ginger molasses cookie for Billy— they found a couple of comfy chairs by the fireplace and settled in.

Billy set the cookie on the table between them.

Charlotte wrapped both hands around her mug, sighing happily at the warmth.

"Don't you own a pair of gloves?" Billy asked.

"None that are rated to a Montana winter," she told him.

"Well, I'm glad to see you're at least wearing a warmer coat than what you had on the other day."

"I borrowed this one from my mom," she confided. "And the boots. I didn't think to pilfer a pair of gloves. Or a hat."

"I guess you don't get weather like this in the Bahamas."

"Not too often," she said, tongue-in-cheek.

One side of his mouth kicked up in what was almost a half smile.

"In case I haven't mentioned it before, it's good to see you, Charlotte."

"You definitely haven't mentioned it," she said. "In fact, I got the impression that you were anything but happy to see me at the career fair last Saturday."

"I was surprised to see you," he admitted. "I hadn't heard that you were back in town."

"I'd only arrived two days before that—and happened to run into Michelle Lovett on day one, which is how I ended up at the career fair."

"You threw that presentation together in two days?"

She shook her head. "Most of it was on my laptop. I just had to get the display materials printed."

"Do you do a lot of educational stuff like that then?"

"I do a lot of everything," she said. "But education is one of my favorite parts of the job."

He grinned. "Questions about dolphin sex notwithstanding?"

"There's always one," she told him. "And while I didn't mention it to the class yesterday, the results of a fairly recent study indicate that dolphins have sex not just for procreation but also for pleasure."

"Seriously?"

She nodded. "Despite the fact that they can only conceive at certain times, they have sex year-round. They've also been observed probing each other's genitals with their flukes, flippers and snouts. And I'm just realizing that this probably isn't an appropriate topic of conversation…for morning coffee."

"Or with someone who has…probed your genitals?"

"Another reason to change the topic," she acknowledged, aware that her cheeks were burning.

"So how long have you been living in the Bahamas?" he asked, taking her cue.

"Technically, I live in Florida, but my research has been focused in and around the Bahamas for the past seven years."

"That must be tough," he remarked wryly. "Turquoise waters and sandy beaches."

She laughed. "It doesn't suck, that's for sure."

"It's certainly a world away from here."

"And not for everyone," she acknowledged.

"You mean me," he guessed.

She shrugged. "You never wanted to be anywhere but here—raising cattle like your dad and your granddad before you. And you got what you wanted, too."

"Yeah," he agreed, though without much enthusiasm.

"I heard about your divorce," she said softly. "I'm sorry."

"That did suck."

"I can imagine."

"It's hard—letting go of someone who's been part of your life for so long," he clarified.

Was he still talking about his now ex-wife? she wondered.

Or was he maybe thinking about their history?

"You were married…" She paused, trying to remember how much time had passed after their aborted nuptials before she'd heard about his wedding. "Eighteen years?"

He nodded.

"That is a long time."

"But not nearly as long as the forever I thought we were signing up for when we exchanged our vows."

She lifted her cup to sip her coffee. "How are your kids dealing with the divorce?"

"It's been an adjustment for all of us," he confided. "The house just feels so different with Jane gone."

"You must miss her a lot."

"I do," he agreed. "Though probably not as much as I should—or maybe not in the way that I should."

She sipped her coffee again, waiting for him to explain.

"I miss having company at the end of the day. I miss having someone to schedule the kids' activities. But the fact of the matter is, we'd kind of been living separate lives for a lot of years. Jane was busy with Branson, Nicky and Jill, and I was busy with the animals, and we lost touch with one another."

"I'm sorry," she said again.

"What about you?" he asked now. "Are you married?"

He pushed half of the cookie across the table to her.

The gesture was automatic—likely because sharing food was something they'd done countless times in the past, though not in a very long time—so she didn't want to reject his overture.

She shook her head as she broke off a piece of the cookie.

"Have you ever been married?"

"No," she said. "The transient nature of my job doesn't really lend itself to putting down roots."

"Roots don't hold very well in sand, anyway," he pointed out.

She smiled at that, before venturing to confide, "I almost got married once."

"Did you?" His tone was politely curious.

She nodded. "A very long time ago, I was engaged to a terrific guy."

"What happened?"

"It's a little embarrassing to admit this," she said. "But I was young and scared and… I left him at the altar."

Understanding dawned in his gaze.

"Probably more embarrassing for him," he said dryly.

"Probably," she acknowledged.

"So why'd you do it?" he asked. "Couldn't you talk to him? Tell him how you were feeling?"

Of course, they both knew that what he was really asking was, *"Why didn't you talk to me?"*

And she was grateful to finally have the chance to explain.

"I should have. I wanted to. But both of our families were pressuring us to marry and—" She swallowed, the pain—and guilt—of the loss of their baby not forgotten, even so many years later. "And I'd recently suffered a miscarriage and…all the emotions I was feeling were just too overwhelming."

"Maybe you should talk to him now," Billy suggested.

"Do you think he'd understand?" she asked hopefully.

"I'm sure, with the wisdom of hindsight, he'd likely agree that seventeen is too young to make a lifetime commitment. He might even say that it all worked out for the best—because you got to pursue dreams you wouldn't have been able to pursue as a teenage wife and mother."

She nodded again and popped another piece of cookie in her mouth.

"It's entirely possible that he might also acknowledge playing a part in your decision to flee the scene of your intended wedding by dismissing your concerns and only hearing what he wanted to hear."

"I'm not sure if he's that evolved," she said lightly.

"Maybe he was so in love with you that he couldn't wait to start your life together—and didn't anticipate that pushing for too much too soon would push you away."

"Do you think he hates me now?"

Billy was silent for a long minute, as if giving real consideration to her question, and she felt the breath back up in her lungs as she waited for his answer.

"No," he finally said, emphasizing his response with a shake of his head. "I'm sure he doesn't hate you."

"That's good then," she said, relieved and grateful and maybe just a little bit sad that they were finally having this heart-to-heart conversation, even if it was in the third person.

He lifted his mug and swallowed a mouthful of coffee.

"Well, enough about my sad romantic history," she said. "Tell me how you met your wife."

"Ex-wife," he reminded her. "You're not the only one with a sad romantic history."

"Okay, so maybe we don't have to talk about her," Charlotte noted. "But can I tell you that I'm happy you finally got the family you always dreamed of having?"

He nodded. "And thank you. My kids really do make every day worth living." His phone chimed to indicate receipt of a text message. Billy glanced at the screen, then lifted his mug to drain the last of his coffee. "And now I really need to be going."

Charlotte nodded. "I've got things to do, too."

"Only twelve days until Christmas," he told her.

"Counting the days, are you?"

"I try not to," he said. "But Sadie has a sign on the door that's kind of hard to miss."

They walked out of the coffee shop together.

"So how long are you going to be in Bronco?" he asked.

"Just until after the New Year."

He nodded. "Well, it was really good to see you again, Charlotte."

"You, too."

He leaned in for a hug as she moved to kiss his cheek. It was awkward.

They each drew back.

"Do you think it's possible that we could someday be friends again?" Charlotte ventured to ask.

"I'd like that," Billy said.

Maybe she should have left it at that, but before she could question the wisdom of saying anything more, the words were spilling out of her mouth. "I've got two tickets to the 'Sounds of the Season' concert at the high school tomorrow night," she said. "Vanessa John gave them to me."

"I've got three tickets of my own," he told her. "For me and Branson and Jill."

"Nicky must be in the band," she realized.

He nodded. "Percussion."

She smiled. "I remember that you played around with the drums when you were in high school, too."

"Nicky does more than play around," he said. "His music teacher says he's got real talent. And thankfully, his interest in music is one thing that hasn't waned since me and Jane split up."

"Then maybe I'll see you at the concert tomorrow night," she said.

"Maybe."

"And maybe, if you want to have coffee again sometime, you could give me a call." She handed him a business card with her cell phone number on it.

"Maybe I will."

Maybe was hardly a guarantee of anything, Charlotte acknowledged, as she walked across the street again to Sadie's Holiday House. But it was a possibility—and the possibility of seeing Billy again made her heart happy.

They'd had a good talk, she thought. Finally cleared the air about their past. And maybe (there was that word again!) taken the first step back toward being friends. Except that she didn't think a woman was supposed to get tingles when she was in the company of a friend— and there were very definitely tingles when she was with Billy.

But she could—and would—ignore her body's instinctive reaction if it meant being able to put the past behind them and move on.

She reached for the door handle and spotted the sign that Billy had mentioned.

12 Days Until Christmas.

Less than two weeks.

Yikes.

She pulled open the door and a musical chime, like the sound of sleigh bells, announced her entrance as she stepped over the threshold.

The store wasn't packed, but there were several customers milling around—a surprising number for the middle of the day in the middle of the week.

Or perhaps not a surprising number, considering that there were only twelve days until Christmas.

Charlotte wasn't entirely sure what she was looking for, but Holiday House had been one of her favorite places to shop when she was a kid—because it was Christmas inside every day of the year. Yes, Valentine's Day got a lot of love in February, Easter décor bloomed in the spring and Halloween put in a ghoulish appearance in the fall, but the shop always smelled like apple cider and gingerbread—two of Charlotte's favorite holiday scents—and much of the space was decorated with Christmas trees and garlands and ornaments all year round.

"Can I help you find anything?" The woman who asked the question had long, wavy blond hair, dark brown eyes and a warm smile.

"I was looking for the Christmas spirit," Charlotte

admitted, her lips curving into a smile. "I think I've found it."

The other woman laughed. "I'm happy to hear you say that, but if you decide you're looking for anything in particular, just let me know. I'm Sadie, and I might be able to steer you in the right direction."

"Thank you, Sadie."

Almost an hour later, Charlotte walked out of the shop with four bags in-hand and a burgeoning friendship with the charming shopkeeper.

"How come you're wearing a tie?" Branson asked, watching in the mirror as his dad wrestled with the accessory.

"Because it's a dress-up occasion," Billy said.

"Is Nicky wearing a tie?"

"He is," Billy confirmed, secretly wishing that he could get away with a zipper-style tie like the one his younger son had donned as part of his band uniform, along with black pants and a white dress shirt.

"Do *I* have to wear a tie?" Branson asked.

"No, but you could take off that hoodie and put on a nice sweater."

A sweater was apparently a reasonable request, because Branson went to do his bidding without further comment.

Jill stomped down the hall wearing a green velvet dress with long sleeves and a skirt that twirled above her knees with black tights and black Doc Martens boots.

"There's my girl," he said.

She answered with a scowl.

"And such a pretty smile," he couldn't resist adding.

Her scowl deepened.

Aside from her expression of displeasure, she really did look nice—and more like a young lady than a little girl these days, which made him both proud and a little regretful, too.

Damn, this single parenting stuff was hard.

But he managed to herd them into his vehicle and get them to the school—forty-five minutes before the program was scheduled to begin because that's what time the musicians were required to be there.

Which meant that, fifteen minutes later and still thirty before curtain, Jill was already bored.

And then Charlotte showed up.

"Miss Taylor!" His daughter's whole demeanor changed when she spotted the marine biologist, who apparently held some kind of superhero status in her eyes.

Charlotte made her way over to them, and Billy introduced her to Branson.

"What are you doing here?" Jill asked.

"I haven't been to one of these events in a long time," Charlotte confided. "But I remembered that the high school band always put on a good holiday concert, so I thought I'd check it out."

"The senior band's pretty good," Branson acknowledged. "The junior band—"

Billy cleared his throat—*loudly*—lest his son say something negative that might be overheard by a friend or family member of someone in the group he suspected was about to be disparaged.

"—isn't the senior band," Branson concluded.

Billy winked at him, grateful for his tact.

"Are you here by yourself?" he asked Charlotte, because she'd mentioned having two tickets to the event.

"I am," she confirmed.

"Would you like to sit with us?" Jill immediately piped up to ask.

"Is that okay with you?" she asked Billy.

He shrugged. "Sure."

"In that case, yes," she responded to Jill. "I would like to sit with you."

They relinquished their tickets at the door and made their way into the auditorium. Branson went first, followed by Billy and Charlotte—until Jill squeezed past to seat herself between the adults.

Charlotte didn't let herself feel disappointed. It was really only luck that she'd run into them in the foyer and was sitting with them at all. And sitting beside Jill was preferable to being surrounded by a bunch of people she didn't know and were likely to ask if she had a son or daughter who was performing in the program.

A reasonable question, and one that wouldn't faze her on most days, but since she'd been spending time with her infant niece, Charlotte had been thinking a lot about the baby she'd lost and she didn't need to make herself the subject of fresh gossip by crying on a stranger's shoulder at the high school holiday concert.

The program opened with the choir singing "Ma'oz Tzur" followed by "The First Noel" and "A Kwanzaa Song." After the choir came junior band, then guitar club, with the drama club performing short skits in between acts while the musicians were exiting or entering the stage. At the midpoint of the show, there was an intermission with snacks and drinks.

Branson loaded up on cookies and found a group of friends to hang with during the break. Jill chose a frosted brownie with red and green sprinkles and washed it down with apple juice. Billy lamented the absence of coffee but settled for a can of cola.

Charlotte casually perused the crowd as she nibbled on a snowflake-shaped sugar cookie when her gaze clashed with that of Bonnie Abernathy.

She hadn't considered that Billy's parents might show up for the concert, and she should have. As Nicky's grandparents, they'd naturally want to watch him perform. But even if she'd anticipated seeing them, she would not have predicted the animosity evident in Bonnie's glare.

The woman who'd once treated her like a daughter, who Charlotte had believed would be her mother-in-law and a grandmother to her child, was looking at her with such open hostility, it made her feel a little queasy.

No longer hungry, she wrapped the remnants of her cookie in a paper napkin and dropped it into the trash bin.

Clearly Bonnie didn't approve of Charlotte being here with her son.

Not that she was *with* Billy, but his mother didn't know that.

Asa was standing beside his wife, but he was either oblivious or indifferent to Charlotte's presence, for which she was grateful.

"I'm gonna go say hi to Grandma and Grandpa," Jill

said, dropping her empty cup in the trash before skipping off to do just that.

"Maybe I should leave," Charlotte said.

"You're not seventeen years old, anymore. You don't need to be intimidated by my mother," Billy said, proving that he wasn't oblivious to Bonnie's contemptuous stare.

"I'm getting the impression she hasn't forgiven me for walking out on our wedding."

"It's been twenty years," he noted. "Past time for her to get over it."

"Easy for you to say. She's not mad at you."

"Of course not. I gave her three grandchildren."

The words were barely out of his mouth when he winced, as if belatedly remembering that she'd carried Bonnie's first grandchild, if only for a very short time.

"I'm sorry," he said, sounding sincerely contrite. "I wasn't—"

She shook her head to cut off his apology, wishing it was as easy to cut the ache out of her heart. "Like you said, it's been twenty years."

"That doesn't mean I've forgotten," he said gently.

"Me, neither." She brushed her hands down the front of her dress. "I'm going to wash up before we head back inside."

"I'll wait for you here."

"You don't have to do that," she protested.

"I'll wait for you here," he said again, in a tone that she imagined brooked no argument when he used it on his kids.

Charlotte had no trouble finding the girls' washroom,

as it was in the same place it had been when she was a student here, and she was washing her hands when Billy's mom walked in.

"I'm surprised to see you here, Charlotte."

"Hello, Mrs. Abernathy."

Billy's mom didn't return her greeting, saying instead, "I hadn't heard that you were back in town."

"Just for the holidays."

"So why are you here with Billy?"

"I'm not with him," she said. "I just happened to run into him and Branson and Jill when I arrived, and Jill invited me to sit with them."

Bonnie frowned at that. "How do you know my granddaughter?"

"I met her at the career fair last weekend."

The older woman's lips thinned as she considered this information.

Charlotte dried her hands, and pretended they weren't shaking. She'd never enjoyed confrontation, and she particularly disliked being in conflict with people she cared about. And despite the fact that she hadn't seen Billy's mom in twenty years, it still hurt to be treated so coolly by the woman she'd once thought of as a second mother.

"Was there anything else?" she asked politely.

"Yes." Bonnie straightened her shoulders. "Billy's had a rough year—and more than enough heartache for one lifetime. He doesn't need you hanging around and messing with him again."

"I'm not. I wouldn't."

"History would suggest otherwise," Bonnie said, and turned on her heel to walk out.

The words were like a dagger to her heart, but she managed to draw in a breath and say, "Mrs. Abernathy, wait."

The other woman turned around slowly.

"I've apologized to Billy for the way I handled things…way back when," Charlotte said. "But I owe you and Mr. Abernathy an apology, too, and I want you to know that I am sorry."

"Water under the bridge," Bonnie said brusquely. "Let's just make sure it stays there."

Charlotte nodded.

Message received.

Chapter Seven

"How was the concert?" Imogen asked her daughter over breakfast the next morning.

"It was good." Charlotte sipped her coffee. "Mostly."

"They really shouldn't make the freshman class perform," her mom said, shaking pepper onto the egg-white omelet that her cook Lina had prepared. "Some of those kids are downright awful—and I say that as a mother who had to listen to her daughter perform."

"I wasn't so bad," she protested.

"There were others who were worse," Imogen allowed.

"Well, I wasn't actually referring to the performances—which were great, by the way," Charlotte said. "I was referring to my encounter with Bonnie Abernathy."

"Oh, dear," Imogen said.

She nodded. "Apparently she still hasn't forgiven me for leaving Billy at the altar."

"It was an emotional day for all of us."

"For me, too," Charlotte felt compelled to remind her mother.

"I know that, darling," Imogen said in a placating tone. "But you were the one who decided to leave while the rest of us were left wondering what happened."

"What happened is that I was seventeen years old and freaking out about the fact that I was going to become Mrs. Billy Abernathy before I'd had a chance to figure out who Charlotte Taylor was."

"I understand that you were young. And I'll admit that your father and I didn't hear you when you tried to tell us you weren't ready to get married."

"Oh, Dad heard me—loud and clear. Because he said that if I was old enough to make a baby, I was old enough to be a wife and mother."

"Your father does have strong opinions," Imogen acknowledged, gesturing for Charlotte to eat her eggs before they got cold.

"I know." She picked up her fork. "I guess I just hoped that you would take my side."

"I didn't realize there were sides to be taken. You told us that you loved Billy and wanted to marry him."

"That was before I lost the baby. Not that I stopped loving him afterward," Charlotte hastened to explain. "But I wasn't quite as eager to become Mrs. Billy Abernathy and give up any opportunity to live my own life."

"That's a little melodramatic, don't you think?"

"Is it? Because I can pretty much guarantee that I

wouldn't have become a marine biologist if I'd gone through with the wedding."

"Your new husband might not have been thrilled by the idea of you attending college seven hundred miles away," Imogen admitted. "But you could have chosen a different focus at a nearby college."

"Like you did?"

Her mother's gaze sharpened. "What is that supposed to mean?"

"Just that you graduated from Great Falls College with an accounting degree, then you married Thaddeus Taylor and had six kids."

"Maybe that doesn't seem like a lot to you, but it was more than enough to keep me busy when those six kids were young," Imogen assured her.

"I know you were busy," Charlotte said. "But were you happy?"

"I was. I am. And I'm sorry that you ever thought differently and decided that your main goal in life should be to not end up like your mother."

"That isn't what I meant at all," she protested. "I only meant that I wanted to do more than be a wife and mother."

"You've certainly done that," Imogen said. "And perhaps, in doing so, missed out on the opportunity to discover how fulfilling those roles can be."

Then she balled up her cloth napkin, pushed away from the table and walked out.

The unexpectedly harsh words exchanged with her mother had taken Charlotte's appetite. But she forced herself to finish eating the breakfast Lina had cooked, because she suspected that her next meal with her mother was going to be crow.

Billy stared at the contents of his refrigerator, considering his dinner options. Though the appliance was fully stocked, nothing appealed to him. Or maybe it was the idea of cooking for one person that didn't appeal to him.

Maybe he'd make a grilled cheese sandwich.

That was easy enough.

And then what?

Was he going to mope around the house all night because it was too damn quiet without the kids stomping around and bickering with one another?

It wasn't his idea of a fun evening, but he had to accept that it was what his life—or at least every other weekend—was going to be now that Branson, Nicky and Jill would be splitting their time between the ranch and their mom's new house.

That was his new reality.

And it really, really sucked.

Of course, he could also go out—head into town for a bite and a beer at Doug's.

He considered inviting Jace to go with him, but since meeting Tamara and taking custody of little Frankie, his youngest brother was all about quiet nights at home. The odds of getting Theo out were usually better, but he'd mentioned plans to meet with a guy he wanted to interview for his "This Ranching Life" podcast.

Instead, Billy pulled out his cell phone and scrolled through the contact listings, looking for someone who might be available on short notice to meet him.

The problem was that most of his friends were married and their wives were unlikely to appreciate being abandoned on a Friday night—and that was if any of them were even willing to venture out of their cozy homes and away from their loving families to hang with a recently divorced friend.

And maybe, if you want to have coffee again sometime, you could give me a call.

Charlotte's words echoed in his head, tempting him.

Things had been a little awkward between them when they'd first sat down in Bean & Biscotti, but once they started talking, the years and the distance seemed to melt away. And everything had been good at the concert the night before—at least until he inadvertently made reference to the baby they'd lost. But Charlotte didn't seem to hold it against him, and she'd been friendly enough when they parted ways—after a hasty goodbye that he knew had more to do with wanting to avoid a confrontation with his mother than him.

He pulled her business card out of his wallet and stared at it for a long minute before he finally dialed the number.

Though Charlotte had given Billy her number, she hadn't actually expected him to use it. Especially not after last night, when it had been apparent to both of them that his mother was not in favor of him spending time with his long-ago fiancée.

But when her cell phone rang late Friday afternoon, the display showing an unfamiliar number, her heart skipped a beat in hopeful anticipation.

She swiped to connect the call. "Hello?"

"Hi, Charlotte. It's Billy."

As if she hadn't immediately recognized his voice.

And as if her heart hadn't skipped another beat when she did, then begun to race.

Still, she managed to respond in a casual tone. "It's good to hear from you."

"You gave me your card," he reminded her. "Told me to call if I wanted to meet for coffee sometime."

"Is that why you're calling? You want to meet for coffee?"

"Actually, I was thinking maybe dinner rather than coffee."

"Dinner," she echoed.

"I know it's really short notice, and you probably have other plans, but—"

"No other plans," she interjected to assure him.

"So you're free to have dinner with an old friend?"

"I'm free," she said.

Free, and perhaps the teensiest bit disappointed that his invitation to dinner was only that and not a date.

But of course he wasn't asking her on a date.

The ink was barely dry on his divorce papers.

And, like his mom had said the night before, he'd had a tough year—and more than enough heartache to last a lifetime.

"That's great," he said, sounding as if he really meant it. "The kids are at their mom's this weekend and the house is far too quiet without them."

"Happy to help," she said, pretending it didn't sting a little to discover that he was motivated by desperation to get out of the house rather than desire to see her.

But she *was* happy to help. To be his friend.

And she could use a friend, too, instead of being a third wheel hanging around with her sister and her new boyfriend. Or—even worse—hanging around with her parents, which was why she was back at Eloise's hotel suite.

"Great. Should I pick you up at the Triple T around seven?"

"Actually, I'm staying at the Heights Hotel with Eloise right now, so it might be easier if I just meet you at the restaurant."

"I'll pick you up," he insisted.

As if it *was* a date.

But it wasn't.

"I'll be waiting in the lobby at seven," she promised.

"I'll see you then."

She disconnected the call, then nearly dropped the phone as her sister's voice startled her.

"Was that Billy?"

Charlotte whirled around. "Is Merry down for her nap already?"

"She is," Eloise confirmed. "Now answer my question."

"Yes, it was Billy," she admitted. "But how did you know?"

"Because you were smiling when you disconnected the call."

"I smile a lot," Charlotte said. "I'm generally a happy person."

"And even happier now that you've got a date with Billy tonight," her sister guessed.

"It's not a date."

"He's picking you up at seven…for dinner?"

She nodded.

"How is that not a date?"

"Because he specifically said *dinner with an old friend.*"

"Hmm." Eloise pursed her lips thoughtfully. "So what are you planning to wear to this dinner that isn't a date?"

Charlotte glanced down at the ratty UW sweatshirt and faded jeans she'd put on that morning. "Can I raid your closet?"

"I already told you that you could. Anytime," her sister reminded her. "But before you start rifling through it, let me show you something."

She slipped into the bedroom and returned with a V-neck cashmere sweater dress in a gorgeous shade of grayish-blue.

"What do you think?"

"It's beautiful," Charlotte said, stroking a hand over the soft fabric.

"Try it on," Eloise urged.

Since Dante was out, Charlotte didn't hesitate to strip off her sweatshirt and jeans and pull the dress over her head.

"I think this is the best thing I've ever felt against my skin," she said, as she smoothed the skirt over her hips.

"Spoken like a woman who hasn't enjoyed the touch of a man in a very long time," her sister teased.

"A very, very long time," she agreed. She turned to face her sister. "What do you think?"

"I think you look stunning. But see for yourself," she said, steering Charlotte toward the full-length mirror on the back of the bathroom door.

She turned to examine her reflection from various angles.

"Well?" Eloise prompted.

"I'm just worried that the neckline is a little low for December in Montana."

"I don't think you're going to be dining al fresco anywhere."

"It might also be a little low for dinner-that's-not-a-date."

"Don't let yourself be limited by someone else's labels," her sister said.

"That's good life advice, but not really applicable to this evening."

"Do you have a different bra?" Eloise asked.

"What? Why?"

"Because that one does nothing to enhance your assets."

"Maybe that's because my assets are…limited."

"Hold that thought." Eloise went back to her bedroom again and returned with a satin-and-lace bra with very defined cups.

"No."

"I bet it will fit you—we were similar sizes before I got baby boobs. And since I've got the baby boobs and am only wearing nursing bras these days, you're welcome to borrow it."

"I don't mind sharing clothes, but I'm not sharing underwear," Charlotte told her sister firmly. "I also don't want to give Billy the impression that I think this is something more than a couple of friends sharing a meal, so there's no reason to enhance my limited assets."

"Or maybe you don't want to let yourself hope that this could be something more than a couple of friends sharing a meal," Eloise said.

"That, too," she agreed.

"It's your call." Her sister returned the bra to her bedroom. "But I say, if you want him, you should go for it."

"It's not that simple," Charlotte said, almost sorry that it wasn't. "I'm only going to be in town until the New Year."

"That's more than two weeks away," Eloise pointed out. "A lot can happen in two weeks."

"Unless an ocean suddenly appears in the middle of Montana, I don't think so."

Her sister's brow furrowed. "Are you really happy traipsing around the globe?" she asked gently. "Do you honestly never think about coming home?"

"The nature of my job means that coming home isn't really an option."

"Which doesn't actually answer my question," Eloise said. "Or maybe it does."

"I made my choice a long time ago," Charlotte reminded her.

Her sister nodded, resigned. "So maybe tonight you should forget about everything else and concentrate on having a good time."

"I can do that," she agreed.

"And don't knock when you come back," Eloise said. "Merry had a rough night last night, so we'll probably be in bed early tonight."

"I won't knock," she promised.

"Good. Now let's see if we can do something with your hair."

She was waiting in the lobby at seven o'clock and immediately made her way outside when she saw Billy's truck pull up in front.

"You're prompt," he noted, hurrying to open the passenger door for her.

"Should I have kept you waiting?"

"No," he said. "I'm just pleasantly surprised. Whenever we have plans to go somewhere, I'll give Jill a time that's half an hour earlier than I actually want to be leaving, to ensure that we're out the door on time."

"Teenage girls are under a lot of pressure to look good all the time," Charlotte told him.

"Are you saying that she'll grow out of it?"

"I don't know if she will, but I have. Or maybe it's just that my wardrobe is much more limited these days, so deciding what to wear isn't a big decision."

"I like what you're wearing tonight," he said.

"I'm wearing knee-high boots and a long coat—you can't even see what I'm wearing."

"I can see enough to know it's a skirt. Or a dress."

"It is a dress," she confirmed. "And not part of my limited wardrobe. I borrowed it from Eloise."

"I was hoping to borrow a sweater from Jace," he said. "But he's rather proprietary about his clothing."

She narrowed her gaze. "You're yanking my chain, aren't you?"

"Maybe. Just a little."

"And maybe I deserve it," she said. "Coming back to Bronco for the holidays without considering the inadequacies of my wardrobe."

"You said 'coming back to Bronco,'" he noted. "Do you not consider Bronco home anymore?"

"I'm not really sure," she admitted. "I've been gone for more years than I lived here, but there's not really anywhere else that I would consider home, either."

"The ocean?"

She laughed. "I spend a fair amount of time in the water, but I'm not actually a mermaid."

"I just realized… I probably should have asked if you ate fish before I made reservations at a seafood restaurant," he said, sounding worried.

"There's a seafood restaurant in Bronco?"

"Nah." He grinned. "I'm just yanking your chain again."

She couldn't resist smiling back, pleased he was feeling comfortable enough to tease her now.

"So where are we going for dinner?" she asked.

"Pastabilities. Have you been there before?"

"It doesn't sound familiar," she said. "But I'm guessing… Italian?"

He turned into the restaurant parking lot. *"Cibo delizioso."*

"Well, look who's suddenly cosmopolitan."

He grinned again. "I know a few key phrases in a few different languages."

"Most of them curse words, I'd bet."

"And you'd win that bet." He maneuvered into a vacant spot.

She reached for the door handle when he put the vehicle into Park, and he immediately instructed her to "stay put," warning that the pavement might be icy.

She didn't generally appreciate being told what to do—or not to do—but with Billy, she knew he was looking out for her, because that's the kind of guy he was. So when he helped her out of the truck and offered his arm, she didn't hesitate to take it.

And if the sense of déjà vu made her heart ache, it was only because she'd missed sharing easy moments like this with her longtime friend. At least that's what she told herself—and very nearly managed to convince herself it was true.

Chapter Eight

He should have stayed home and made a sandwich, Billy mused, as he helped Charlotte out of her coat. Because despite his invitation to "dinner with an old friend," being with her was starting to feel like a date.

It wasn't an uncomfortable feeling.

To the contrary, it felt perfectly natural—like something they'd done a hundred times before. Possibly because they had done it a hundred times before, though when they'd been dating in high school their budget had usually limited them to burgers and fries or sharing popcorn at a movie.

"Nice place," she said, looking around the restaurant. *"Bel ristorante."*

"Now who's cosmopolitan?"

She grinned. "When you spend a lot of time on a boat

with researchers from other countries, you can't help but pick up some of their language."

"Including curse words?"

"Absolutely."

A server appeared then. After introducing himself as Stefano, he filled their glasses with water, recited the daily specials and asked if they wanted anything else to drink while they perused the menus.

Charlotte opted for a glass of pinot noir; Billy upgraded the order to a half carafe.

A few minutes later, Stefano returned with the wine and a basket of warm bread. He poured a splash of wine into Billy's glass for him to sample and approve, which he did, conscious of Charlotte watching him closely.

"Did I do it wrong?" he asked, after the server had taken their orders and left them alone again.

"I wouldn't know," she said. "I'm hardly a connoisseur."

"So what were you thinking while he was pouring the wine?"

"Just that this is new territory for us. The last time we shared a meal together, we were probably sipping soda in paper cups."

"You're probably right," he noted. "We weren't even old enough to drink yet when we were planning to get married."

"I remember that my dad ordered a case of sparkling grape juice for the toasts. Just for us—because you can bet that the parents were going to be drinking the real stuff."

He managed to smile as he reached into the basket

for a slice of bread. "We really were ridiculously young, weren't we?"

She nodded.

He buttered the bread, offered it to her.

She shook her head. "No, thanks."

He shrugged and bit into the slice, watching her across the table as he chewed.

"Now you're staring," she said.

"Sorry," he said, unable to deny that he'd been doing just that. "I guess I wasn't expecting…you look really great."

She lifted a brow. "You weren't expecting me to look great?"

He felt the tips of his ears burn, as they always did when he was embarrassed. "You'd think I'd have trouble fitting my size twelve feet in my mouth, but apparently not."

She laughed softly. "You thought I'd be wearing jeans and a Dolphin Harbour Project T-shirt?"

"Maybe."

"I wasn't wearing jeans and a dolphin T-shirt last night," she reminded him.

"That's true. And you looked good last night, too. Not that you don't look good in jeans and a T-shirt," he hastened to clarify.

"You might want to get that foot out of your mouth before your dinner comes," she teased.

"Will I only push it in deeper if I say there's something different about your hair tonight, too?"

"No," she said. "And that was my sister again. Eloise didn't think my usual ponytail worked with the dress."

"I like the ponytail," he said. "But this looks good, too." Her hair had been styled into loose curls that framed her face and spilled over her shoulders, tempting a man to run his fingers through them.

"It was kind of fun, letting her do my hair and makeup," Charlotte told him now. "We never did any of that stuff together when we were growing up, because she was still a kid when I left town."

"You were still a kid, too," he noted.

"Maybe. Technically. But I didn't feel like a kid. At least, not when I left." She lifted her glass of wine, sipped. "By the time I got to Seattle and realized how far away from home I was, and completely on my own, I felt like a kid again. Scared and alone and wanting nothing more than my parents to show up and rescue me."

"So why didn't you come home?"

She shrugged. "I must have inherited some of my father's stubbornness."

"Manicotti di ricotta for the lady. And chicken parmigiana for the gentleman." Stefano set their plates in front of them, then went through the usual routine of offering freshly grated parmesan and ground pepper.

For the next several minutes, they focused on their food. When Charlotte paused to sip her wine, she said, "This place is definitely a new favorite."

"I've never been disappointed by a meal here," Billy agreed. "DJ's Deluxe is another new restaurant you should try, if you haven't already."

"I haven't," she said.

"We'll go there next time." And then, when his words registered, he immediately tried to backtrack. "Not that

I expect we'll be doing this again. I mean, we could. If you wanted to."

"I'm not opposed to doing this again," she told him.

"Well, good."

Charlotte nibbled another bite of manicotti before she ventured to ask, "Did your parents say anything to you about me being at the concert last night?"

"No," he said. "Although I didn't really talk to them today. Why? Did they say something to you?"

"I crossed paths with your mom, and she let it be known that she didn't think us spending time together was a good idea."

"I'm sorry."

She shrugged. "I can hardly blame her for feeling that way."

"I'm thirty-seven years old," he pointed out. "I hardly need my parents' permission to hang out with an old friend."

There it was again—the reminder to both of them that they were just friends hanging out together. That this wasn't a date.

"I have no objection to us being friends," Charlotte said. "But I really wish you'd stop throwing the word *old* around."

"I didn't mean old in reference to age," he told her. "Just that we go way back."

"That we do," she agreed. "Even if we lost touch for a lot of years."

"Did you keep in touch with any of our old—sorry, *former*—group of friends?"

She shook her head. "I tried to. I reached out to Darcy

and Selena a few times, but they both made it clear that I was *persona non grata* for leaving you at the altar."

"I'm sorry for that," he said.

Now she shrugged. "I had to live with the consequences of my choices—at least, that's what my dad said when I told him I was pregnant.

"But I made new friends in Seattle. And in college. Good friends. And though we all seemed to scatter in different directions after graduation, depending on specific areas of interest and job availability, we keep in fairly regular contact."

And if any of those friends happened to be in town and invited her to get together for a meal, she wouldn't hesitate. But sitting across the table from Billy, Charlotte found herself again questioning the wisdom of her decision to accept his invitation. Because while she was always happy to help out a friend—and she did want to be Billy's friend—she wasn't sure her feelings for him could be confined to such a limited description.

Yes, she'd been the one to walk (okay, run) away, but only because she was scared, not because she didn't love him. And while she still believed she'd done the right thing—for both of them—spending time with him now was threatening to bring those old feelings back to the surface, reminding her of the attraction that had always sparked between them.

He was an incredibly handsome man, but more than that, she knew he was a good man. Thoughtful and kind and loyal.

And right now, she could see that he was also unhappy.

"Am I such a horrible dinner companion?"

"What?" He glanced up, surprised by her question. "No. Why would you ask that?"

"Because you're sitting there scowling at your chicken parm."

"I'm sorry," he said. "This was probably a bad idea."

"Dinner with me?"

"Not the *with you* part," he denied.

"Well, the pasta's good," she said.

He twirled his fork in his spaghetti, apparently willing to give it a try.

"Why don't you tell me about your kids?" she suggested.

His scowl deepened. "I don't think that's going to help me forget that they're gone this weekend."

"I didn't ask about them as a distraction, but because I genuinely want to know what they're like."

"Well, you've met Jill a couple times," he pointed out.

She nodded. "Your daughter is a bright and beautiful young lady."

"I think so," he agreed.

"Does she look like her mom?"

His lips twitched. "Should I be insulted that you said she was beautiful and immediately assumed that she takes after her mom?"

"You know I didn't mean it like that," she chided.

"Do I?"

"She has your eyes," Charlotte said. "But her hair is lighter in color and her build more delicate."

"Yes," he agreed. "Lucky for her, she does look like her mom."

"And does it terrify you to think that she's going to lose her heart to some boy like I lost mine to you?"

"I'm worried about more than her heart," he admitted.

"Well, she's young yet."

"And growing up fast."

"She's also smart," Charlotte said. "If that's any comfort."

"Nicky calls her a nosy know-it-all, but I guess that's kind of the same thing."

She smiled. "Do they bicker a lot?"

"Constantly."

"I grew up with three brothers," she reminded him. "I have some sympathy for Jill."

"And I'm sure your brothers would feel sympathy for Branson and Nicky."

"No doubt." She sipped her wine again before venturing to ask, "So how do they feel about spending weekends with their mom?"

"This is the first one," Billy confided. "She only recently moved into a new house. Prior to that, she was in a condo and didn't have room for them to stay over."

"Okay. So how did they feel about spending *this* weekend with their mom?"

"Branson balked at going. Of course, he's seventeen, so he'd rather spend a Friday night hanging out with his friends than on a lawyer-scheduled visit with his mom. Especially as there are a few females in his group of friends, and I think he's got a crush on one of them."

"Seventeen, huh?" she mused, remembering what they'd been doing at the same age.

"Believe me—I've had 'The Talk' with him," Billy said, proving that his mind had gone down the same path.

"The same talk your dad had with you?"

"I like to think I was a little more emphatic. And that I was able to talk to him with a slightly different perspective.

"However, I'm also aware that no amount of talking can compete with the hormones undoubtedly running rampant through his system, so I bought a box of condoms and put it in the cupboard of the bathroom Branson and Nicky share. And I promised I won't ever peek inside to see how many might be missing, but that I would periodically buy a new box."

"A good idea," Charlotte said.

"I thought so, too. But there are now four boxes in the cupboard and Branson told me to stop buying them. He promised that he'd let me know if and when I needed to buy more. Or—'here's an idea,' he said. 'I could actually buy them myself.'"

"Coulda, shoulda, woulda," she mused.

"I do think kids these days are smarter than we were."

"You mean you *hope* kids these days are smarter than we were," she said.

"That's the truth," he agreed.

"Anyway, aside from hanging out with his friends, what does Branson like to do?"

"Sleep in and play video games."

"Does he enjoy working on the ranch?"

"Most days. At least, I think so. He seems to have decided—rather than just accepted—that he's going to be a rancher like his father and his grandfather before him."

"And is that what you want for him?"

"Yes. And no."

She sipped her wine, waiting for him to elaborate.

"Obviously, if we want to keep the ranch in the family, we need some of the next generation to carry it on. But I also think it's important for my kids—and any that my brothers or sisters might have—to have choices. So I made Branson apply to college, because I want him to expand his horizons and explore other options, even if he doesn't see the point in getting a diploma just to continue to do the work he's already doing around the ranch."

"How about Nicky? Does he have any plans for his future? Aspirations of finding fame and fortune as a drummer in a rock band?"

"He's far too practical to imagine anything like that," Billy said. "Thankfully, in addition to music, he has quite an aptitude for numbers."

"A good foundation for a lot of careers," she noted.

"Of course, he figures he's going to be a rancher, too. Which is fine—as long as it's what he wants."

"Sounds like you've got some pretty great kids."

"Yeah," he agreed. "But the divorce has been tough, in different ways, on all of them."

"I'm sure it has."

"And on me, too," he admitted. "One of the reasons I've struggled to get into the holiday spirit this year is that they're going to be with their mom on Christmas Day."

"I'm sorry," she said again.

He shrugged. "Anyway, that's enough about that," he said. "Tell me how it is that you're home for the holidays this year."

"I recently finished a grant proposal for funding to continue our ongoing study of Atlantic spotted and bottlenose dolphins and, since I didn't have any workshops or conferences on my schedule, I decided to spend some time here."

"A grant proposal sounds like paperwork."

She nodded. "Being a marine biologist is about a lot more than swimming with dolphins."

"And how does it feel to be back in Montana? To be surrounded by land?"

"It feels good. And a little weird," she said. "I'm happy to have some time with my family—and friends—but I'd be lying if I said I wasn't itching to get back to work. As much as it's nice to be able to sleep in, I miss feeling as if I have a sense of purpose. And spending time with my father, who's never seen the value in what I do, doesn't help. He never misses an opportunity to question my life choices."

"Thaddeus Taylor is not known for mincing words," he acknowledged.

"I try not to pay him too much attention, because my job is truly amazing. But I can't deny that I feel torn sometimes, because if I continue doing what I'm doing, I'm never going to be able to move back. And if I move back, I won't be able to continue doing the work I love."

"I'd say that puts you right between the proverbial rock and the hard place."

She nodded.

"So tell me how you ended up studying marine biology."

"When I left Bronco, I needed some distance from everything that happened—and didn't happen—and time to sort out my tangled emotions. So I got in my SUV and started driving and ended up in Washington State. Seattle, to be specific."

"Where you got a job at Starbucks," he guessed.

She managed a smile. "Actually, my first job was at a restaurant called Captain Mike's. It was located by the waterfront and packed every night, and I was happy to be busy, to not have time to think…about you…and the baby we lost…and the future I'd thrown away."

She pushed aside the melancholy to move ahead with her story. "But when the weather started to cool and tourism dropped off, resulting in a noticeable decline in my income, I got a second job—at Starbucks."

"For real?"

"For real," she confirmed. "A rite of passage for any young person living in Seattle, at least according to Marissa—a coworker at Captain Mike's who gave me a place to stay and told me about her marine biology studies at U Dub.

"As I'm sure you can imagine, the ocean was a whole new world to someone who'd grown up on a cattle ranch in Montana, and I was immediately captivated by her description of it. And when Marissa asked about my plans for the future, I decided that I wanted to study the underwater world, too.

"Partly because Marissa's enthusiasm was contagious but also partly to retaliate against my father's efforts to control my life. Because I knew that if I became a marine biologist, I'd never have to return to Bronco.

"Of course, at the time, I was too young—and maybe too stubborn—to anticipate that there might come a time when I wanted to come back. That I might actually miss my family. Primarily my brothers and sisters, but eventually my parents, too."

"What did your parents say about your chosen field of study?"

"Nothing good," she admitted. "Then again, they didn't say much at all for the first few months after I left. In fact, my dad was so furious with me for walking out on the wedding and humiliating not just my groom but my own family that he refused to give me any financial support, certain that when I ran out of money, I'd come home.

"He didn't expect me to actually get a job and make plans for my future, and when I got up the courage to tell him that I wanted to go to college in Seattle, he was not impressed. He said that he would be happy to pay for me to go to Montana State or the University of Montana, but no way was he going to pay for me to study marine biology in Washington."

"So you managed to scrape together your tuition working two part-time jobs?"

"Well, I had to put off going to college for a while," she said. "And my mom did help a little bit. She would occasionally deposit small sums of money into my bank account. Never an amount large enough to draw my dad's attention but always enough to ensure I could pay my rent and add a few dollars to my tuition fund.

"So I started at U Dub the following year, just a few weeks after my nineteenth birthday. It took some time to adjust to college life, but I made new friends at school and enjoyed my classes. I was a little surprised to discover how much I really loved studying marine biology, and after a quarter at Friday Harbor Laboratories in the San Juan Islands, I was hooked."

"After my second year, when my dad saw that I was serious about studying marine biology despite the obstacles he put in my path, he finally came through and sent me the money for my tuition. I was tempted to send it back," she confided. "I'd managed to get through the first two years without any help—or not very much—and I felt confident that I could continue to do so. I *wanted* to do so.

"But I knew that if I sent it back, he'd see that as a rejection of his overture and we'd be back to not talking again. So I thanked him and cashed the check, then I divided the money and donated it to Oceana, The Ocean Conservancy, The Coral Reef Alliance and The Wild Dolphin Project." She grinned. "They were all very grateful for his support."

"And, most important, you ended up with a career that you love."

"I feel incredibly lucky to do what I do," she told him.

"I'm glad you're happy," he said.

And she was. Maybe she wasn't living the life she'd once imagined, but it was a good life.

So why was she suddenly wondering about the path not taken?

Chapter Nine

Stefano came by then to take away their dinner plates and offer a dessert menu.

Billy pushed the page across the table to Charlotte first, but she shook her head.

"I couldn't manage another bite of anything," she said regretfully.

"Are you sure? Because they have caramel pecan cheesecake."

Charlotte looked at the server. "Is that true?"

"It's one of our most popular menu items," he confirmed. "Some customers come in just for that."

"Now I'm going to have to try at least a bite," she decided.

Billy grinned. "Some things never change."

"You might be right about that," she agreed.

"Anything for you, sir?" Stefano asked Billy.

"Why don't you bring one slice of cheesecake with two forks and another slice to go?"

"Coffee or tea with your dessert?"

They both opted for coffee—decaf.

"Do you really expect me to share my cheesecake while you hoard your dessert for later?" Charlotte asked Billy when the server had gone.

"I do not," he said. "But I thought you might like to share *my* cheesecake and take yours home for later."

She sighed. "You always did that."

"Did what?"

"Made sure I got the bigger share of my favorite things. The donut with the most sprinkles. The cupcake with the most icing. The last Milk Dud in the box."

"Maybe because I learned, way back in kindergarten, that you take no prisoners when it comes to getting your sugar fix."

They paused their conversation when Stefano returned with their coffee, but Charlotte picked it up again when the server had gone.

"You mean when you tried to steal one of my Little Debbie Swiss Rolls?" she asked Billy.

"They were *my* Little Debbie Swiss Rolls," he said.

She frowned. "I don't think so."

"I know so—because you tackled me for them."

"Oh, yeah." She smiled at the memory. "And then you decided that we could share them—and you gave me the bigger one."

"They're mass produced in a factory to a uniform size," he pointed out. "There wasn't a bigger one."

"You gave me the bigger one," she said again, because whether or not it had actually been bigger, that's how she'd always remembered it.

Because that was the day she'd started to fall in love with Billy Abernathy.

"One caramel pecan cheesecake with two forks," Stefano said, setting the plate—drizzled and dotted with extra caramel sauce—on the table between them, along with a cardboard box. "And one to go."

Charlotte's mouth watered as she stared at the four inches of creamy cheesecake dripping with caramel and topped with candied whole pecans on a graham cracker crust.

"What are you waiting for?" Billy asked, when she picked up a fork but made no move to dig into the dessert.

"It almost looks too good to eat."

"It does look good," he acknowledged. "But until you actually taste it, how will you know if it tastes as good as it looks?"

She slid the tines of the fork into the cake, then lifted the bite to her mouth.

The caramel was sweet and sticky, the pecans were crunchy and nutty, the cheesecake was…heaven.

A blissful sigh hummed in her throat.

"I'm guessing it tastes as good as it looks," he said, sounding amused.

She shook her head. "It's better."

"I'll be the judge of that." He dug into the other end of the cake with his own fork.

Now it really felt like a date.

Despite the fact that they each had their own utensil, sharing food from the same plate seemed…intimate somehow.

How many times had they done something like this in the past? Digging into a plate of nachos from opposite sides or sharing an order of fries from the cafeteria at school or alternating licks of a double-scoop ice cream cone (because it was more ice cream but less costly than two single-scoop cones.)

After a few more bites, Charlotte set her fork down in surrender and pushed the plate toward Billy.

"The rest is all yours," she said. "I won't be able to get out of this dress if I have another bite."

"I could always give you a hand."

The response was automatic. Teasing banter that she knew didn't mean anything.

Just as the image that immediately sprang to mind of Billy helping her out of the dress didn't mean anything. But the heat that spread through her body was all too real.

"I'm sorry." His apology was as automatic as his flirtatious response had been. "I didn't mean—"

"I know you didn't mean anything by it," she said. "Unfortunately."

He held her gaze for a long moment; tension simmered between them.

"Now *I'm* sorry," she said.

"Don't be," he told her. "It's just…really bad timing."

"A common theme of our relationship, it seems."

"But I think we've proven tonight that we can be friends."

She nodded.

"And now I should get you back to your hotel."

He paid the check and helped her with her coat.

There was another moment, when he was standing close, that his gaze lingered on the vee at the front of her dress as she buttoned her coat.

But what did it matter that his gaze lingered when he'd made a point of reminding her—*again*—that friendship was all that was on the table?

Well, that and her dessert.

He picked up the takeout container and offered it to her.

"Wouldn't want you to leave that behind," he said.

"I would have made you come back for it," she told him.

Billy chuckled. "I have no doubt."

He put his hand on her back as he guided her toward the exit, and Charlotte decided that she didn't need a coat—she just needed the heat from his touch to warm her all the way through.

Or maybe not, she amended, as they walked out into the night and cold air enveloped her. "Brr."

He opened the passenger side door for her and helped her into the truck before hurrying around to the driver's side where he cranked up the heat.

"It will warm up soon enough," he promised.

"It's Bronco," she said. "It won't warm up until the spring."

"I meant the truck," he clarified.

"It was seventy-six degrees in the Bahamas today."

"Do you check the weather forecast just to torture yourself?"

"It's more of a habit really," she told him.

"Do you ever check the Bronco forecast when you're in the Bahamas?" he wondered.

"Every day," she confirmed.

"Really?" he asked, surprised.

She shrugged. "When you grow up on a ranch, you quickly learn the importance of the weather—not just temperature but precipitation."

"That's the truth."

"And even when I'm swimming with the dolphins, I wonder if there's been enough rain to grow the grass for the cattle or if the local ranchers had to spread hay for them."

"I guess it's in your blood, even if it's not in your heart."

Except there had been a time, a very long time ago, when she'd been certain that being a rancher's wife was in her future. And she hadn't hated the idea, because she'd loved Billy.

"But you've had an adventurous life, haven't you?" he mused, as he drove away from the restaurant.

"I've been lucky."

"It sounds to me like you've worked hard."

"That, too," she agreed.

"Well, for what it's worth, I'm glad you got to live your own life and see the world," he said. "Things you never would have had a chance to do if you'd walked down the aisle that day."

"Still, I should have handled things differently."

"Which we covered when we had coffee the other day."

"I guess we did," she agreed.

He pulled into the hotel parking lot.

"Well, thanks again for dinner."

"Hold on a second," Billy said. "I'll find a parking spot and walk you to your door."

"That really isn't necessary," Charlotte told him.

"Necessary or not, I was raised to be a gentleman."

"A gentleman would drop me at the door so—"

"So you don't have to walk across the parking lot in the cold?" he interjected, as he pulled up by the front entrance.

"Thank you," she said again.

"I'll meet you inside in just a minute," he promised.

It took him two minutes to park and make his way to the lobby, but she didn't mind waiting, especially when she saw that he'd remembered the box of cheesecake she'd forgotten in his truck.

His steps slowed as he approached, his head moving from side to side to take in his surroundings. Or maybe the extravagant holiday décor, with miles of garland and twinkling lights and a towering tree surrounded by decorative "presents."

"You'd think Christmas was coming the way this place is all decked out," he mused.

"Ten days," she told him.

"Are you planning to stay with your sister the whole time you're in Bronco?"

"No. In fact, I've been splitting my time pretty evenly between here and my parents' place." She pressed the button to summon the elevator. "I feel a little bit like a third wheel here, but I feel a lot like an uninvited guest at the Triple T."

He followed her inside and the doors whooshed shut.

"It's pretty quiet for ten o'clock on a Friday night," he noted.

"I don't think this is the kind of hotel that caters to drunken bachelor parties or tolerates kids running in the halls."

"Then I guess your sister better find other accommodations before her little one starts to run."

"Ha ha," Charlotte said. "Actually, Dante's easing her toward the idea of buying a house, but she wants to take some time to focus on Merry first.

"And the experience of motherhood has already transformed her. My little sister would be the first to admit that she used to hit the snooze button on her alarm clock half a dozen times in the morning, but as soon as Merry makes a peep, she's up to see what she needs."

"People who don't have kids can't understand how having a child changes everything," he agreed. "And there goes my foot in my mouth again."

"Don't apologize again," Charlotte said. "Please."

He nodded.

And she was relieved to move away from the subject of the baby they'd lost, because she didn't want or need his apologies. Especially as he had no reason to feel guilty and she wasn't in any position to absolve him of guilt even if he did. She had yet to forgive herself for the momentary flash of relief she'd felt when she'd realized she was no longer pregnant. Yes, she'd mourned for her child, but she hadn't been ready to be a mom at seventeen.

Of course, she'd thought she would have the opportunity to have a child in the future. That eventually she'd meet someone else, fall in love, get married and have a family.

Instead, she'd fallen in love with dolphins and spent the better part of two decades focused on her work with them. Now she was closer to forty than thirty, had no significant other and no real home.

Her choice, she reminded herself, as they exited the elevator and walked down the hall. Or maybe her punishment for that momentary flash of relief, she acknowledged.

"Apparently the decorations extend past the reception area," Billy remarked, noting that all the guest rooms had garland draped over the doorways and wreaths on the doors. And the larger suites with double doors had two wreaths and potted evergreens with twinkly lights flanking the doors. "All that's missing is Christmas music."

"You mean like what was playing in the lobby?" she asked.

"Was it? I didn't notice," he admitted. "Or maybe I've started to tune it out, because that's all you hear this time of year."

"We listened to 'Yellow' by Coldplay on repeat for hours on end," she reminded him.

"That's good music."

She didn't disagree.

"Well, this is me."

She was surprised to hear her phone ping, indicating receipt of a text message, as she stopped by the door to Eloise's suite. She pulled the device out of the side pocket of her purse, her brows drawing together as she read the message.

Then she tipped her head back to look up and felt a warm flush climb into her cheeks.

"Something wrong?" Billy asked.

"No." She sighed. "Just Eloise playing cupid."

"Isn't she a couple months early for that?"

"Or twenty years too late."

"Huh?"

She shook her head, even as her eyes shifted upward again.

Following her gaze, Billy spotted a sprig of a green plant hanging overhead.

"Is that…mistletoe?" he asked.

"Apparently."

"Did your sister put it there for you…and me?"

"That's what she said," Charlotte admitted, feeling more heat suffuse her face. "But you shouldn't feel… obligated."

"I don't feel obligated," he assured her.

"Well, that's…good."

He took a step closer. "But I do feel tempted."

And apparently he was unable to resist the temptation, because he lowered his head and brushed his mouth over hers.

The moment their lips touched, passion flared, as bright and hot as it had done when they were teenagers.

There was a soft thud as she dropped her purse to

the floor before she lifted her arms to link them around his neck. He broke the kiss only long enough to set the takeout box beside her purse so that his hands were free to unknot the belt at her waist, then make quick work of the buttons that ran down the front of her coat. His hands moved over her torso, tracing her curves through the soft fabric of her dress.

Her hands were inside his coat now, too, reaching under his sweater to discover another layer. She yanked the T-shirt out of his jeans and then her cold hands were on him. He didn't protest, because her touch felt so damn good.

Her lips parted, allowing him to deepen the kiss. Their tongues touched and tangled. Suddenly he felt like he was seventeen again, and ready to spread a blanket in the bed of his pickup truck and stretch out beside her.

But he knew this moment couldn't lead to anything more.

Because he wasn't seventeen. He was a thirty-seven-year-old father of three teenagers—one of whom was seventeen—and the ink was barely dry on his divorce papers. He wasn't ready to get involved with someone new. Or even someone from long ago.

And Charlotte was only going to be in town a short while.

Until the New Year, she'd said.

He'd made the mistake of thinking she would stay once before. He wasn't going to make that mistake again.

With more reluctance than he wanted to acknowledge, he eased his mouth from hers.

He watched as the tip of her tongue touched her top

lip, swollen from his kiss. The pulse point at the base of her jaw was racing, her chest rising and falling with each breath.

"You make me feel like I'm a teenager again," he confided in a gruff tone. "And we weren't very smart as teenagers."

"We're definitely older and wiser now," she said.

His mouth twisted. "Older, anyway."

She managed to smile. "We can blame the mistletoe."

He took a step back.

Away from the mistletoe.

Away from the temptation of Charlotte's kissable lips.

"We'll blame the mistletoe," he agreed.

"Anyway—" she cleared her throat "—thank you again for dinner."

"It was my pleasure."

She picked up the cheesecake and her purse, rummaging through the latter for the key card. He waited until she tapped it against the reader and the door clicked to unlock.

"Good night, Billy."

"Good night, Charlotte."

Then he was alone in the hall, staring at the outside of the closed door.

Well, spending the evening with Charlotte had definitely distracted him from thinking about his kids being with their mom.

Now he just needed something to distract him from thinking about Charlotte.

Chapter Ten

"So…" Eloise said to her sister the next morning. "Did it work?"

"Did what work?" Charlotte asked, sliding a mug into position under the spout of the Keurig.

"The mistletoe."

"You do realize the plant doesn't really have magical powers, don't you?"

"Did he kiss you or not?" her sister pressed.

Charlotte lifted the cup to her lips, sipped cautiously.

"He *did* kiss you," Eloise declared triumphantly.

"I didn't say anything," she protested.

"Exactly."

She sighed. "Okay, yes. He kissed me. But it didn't mean anything."

"Is that what he said?"

"That's what *I'm* saying."

"I know you're not planning on sticking around past the New Year," Eloise admitted. "But that doesn't mean you can't have some fun while you're here, does it?"

"I don't think Billy is looking for fun. The man is still adjusting to being a single father after more than eighteen years of marriage."

"Which is exactly why he should be looking for fun," Eloise said. "Someone to help him forget that his wife left him for another man."

Charlotte nearly choked on a mouthful of coffee. "Is that what happened?"

Her sister frowned. "You didn't know?"

"How would I know something like that?"

Eloise shrugged. "I thought he might have mentioned it. What did you guys talk about, anyway?"

"Apparently everything except why his marriage fell apart," Charlotte realized. "Are you sure that's what happened?"

"I heard it from none other than Robin Abernathy."

Which was almost as good as directly from the horse's mouth, Charlotte knew, because Eloise was responsible for the marketing of "Rein Rejuvenation"— the line of horse therapeutics that Billy's sister had developed.

"Apparently Jane was feeling bored at home, so she decided to take a French class," Eloise continued. "And ended up hooking up with her instructor."

"Ouch." Charlotte could only imagine how that must have stung. "Was Billy devastated?"

"I don't know about devastated, but shocked, for

sure. I guess he had no idea that she was unhappy—in their marriage or their bedroom."

Charlotte felt a little uneasy talking to her sister about her former fiancé's love life—and admittedly curious about his wife's reasons for straying. Because while she and Billy had been young lovers, still learning how to give one another pleasure, she remembered that he'd been unselfish and attentive—and very eager to please. Certainly she hadn't had any complaints.

But who knew what happened after almost two decades of marriage?

She certainly had no experience in that regard.

Whatever reasons his wife had for leaving, they were none of Charlotte's business. But she did have to wonder why, throughout all of their conversations about his family, Billy had failed to mention that his wife had left him for another man.

Perhaps he was embarrassed. She could certainly understand why he wouldn't want everyone in town to know that he'd been cheated on.

A more troubling possibility was that he might still be in love with his ex.

Although he certainly hadn't kissed her last night like a man in love with another woman.

But whether he was or wasn't didn't really matter—there could be no future for them together. She was leaving town soon after the New Year and Eloise's advice about fun aside, Charlotte couldn't imagine ever having a casual hookup with the man she'd once loved with her whole heart.

* * *

Seeing the decorated tree in the lobby of the Heights Hotel reminded Billy that Christmas was coming—whether he was in a celebratory mood or not. If he'd been on his own, he would have forgone decorating altogether, but he wasn't on his own and he wanted to make this holiday as normal as possible for his kids. Which meant a tree in the living room, stockings on the mantel and various other Christmas kitsch around the house.

He was hauling boxes of decorations from the attic Saturday afternoon when there was a knock on the door.

"Mom. What brings you by today?"

"Can I come in?"

"Of course." He stepped away from the door.

She looked at the pile of boxes at the base of the stairs. "You're finally getting ready for Christmas?"

"I can't put it off much longer, can I?"

"Not if you plan to celebrate this year," she agreed.

"Do you want a cup of coffee or something?" he offered, waiting for her to explain the reason for her visit.

She shook her head. "No, thanks. I've got groceries in the car that I need to take home and put away, but I saw your truck as I was driving by and…well, I noticed that your truck wasn't there last night."

"I went out for dinner."

"By yourself?"

"No. With a friend."

Bonnie waited, obviously hoping he would provide more information.

Billy figured she already knew—or at least suspected—the truth, and that was the reason for her pointed questions.

"Was it a date?" she finally asked.

He immediately started to deny the label, then he realized that despite his insistence that they were only two friends sharing a meal, the evening he'd spent with Charlotte had certainly checked off all the boxes—right down to the good-night kiss.

"I guess it was a date," he said.

She frowned. "Don't you think it's a little soon to be dating?"

"The divorce was pretty recent," he acknowledged. "But considering that my ex-wife is already living with her new boyfriend, I don't think it's out of line for me to spend some time in the company of a woman."

"Maybe it's not too soon for you," she said. "But what about the kids? How do you think they'll feel to discover that their dad has moved on?"

"I don't think they'll have any strong opinions on the subject."

"Well, I have some opinions," his mom said.

"I'm shocked."

"Don't you take that tone with me," she admonished.

"I don't mean to be disrespectful," Billy said. "But I'm thirty-seven years old and I don't need your permission to go out on a date—which is exactly what I said to Charlotte last night when she expressed concern that you might disapprove."

"So you *were* with Charlotte," she said, sounding none too happy about the fact.

"You wouldn't be giving me such a hard time if you hadn't already figured that out."

"I suspected," she admitted. "I'd hoped I was wrong."

"You used to love Charlotte."

"That was before she left you standing at the altar."

"Twenty years ago, Mom. Don't you think we should all be over that by now?"

"It was humiliating."

"For me? Or for you?"

She huffed out a breath. "For all of us. And her parents, too. Goodness knows how much money Thaddeus spent on that wedding—and then she just walked out as if none of it—as if *you*—didn't matter."

"How old were you when you got married, Mom?"

She frowned. "What does that have to do with anything?"

"How old?" he asked again.

"Twenty-two," she admitted.

"And at twenty-two, were you at all nervous about making that walk down the aisle? Wondering how your life would change?"

She didn't respond.

"Charlotte was seventeen," he reminded her.

"You were both seventeen," she pointed out. "And you didn't balk at making a commitment."

"Maybe I loved her more than she loved me," he said, a suspicion he'd harbored for twenty years and finally accepted as a fact.

"I know you were heartbroken when she left," Bonnie acknowledged now. "And I don't want to see you get your heart broken again."

"You don't have to worry about me."

"You have three children," she noted. "Let me know when you stop worrying about them."

"Touché."

"Speaking of children," she said, in an obvious effort to shift the topic of conversation, "when are yours going to be home?"

"Tomorrow afternoon."

"Have you heard from them?"

"A couple text messages from Jill, checking in on me."

Bonnie smiled. "She's a good girl."

"Most of the time," he agreed.

"Do you have any plans tonight?"

"Not as of yet." He'd thought about calling Charlotte again, but after the kiss they'd shared the night before, he thought it was probably best to put a little space between them. Get his head screwed on straight and his hormones under control.

"Do you want to come for dinner?" she asked.

He was grateful for the olive branch she was offering, but he couldn't resist teasing, "What are you cooking?"

She lifted a brow. "Does it matter?"

"Not in the least," he assured her.

"Dinner will be on the table at six."

While Billy was having dinner with his parents, Charlotte was doing the same with hers after having moved her suitcase into her old room at the Triple T, where she would be staying for the next few days.

"I see you finally remembered where you live," Thaddeus said, when he came into the dining room and found his eldest daughter seated at the table.

"Thad," his wife said warningly.

"I don't live here," Charlotte said. "I live in Florida."

"But you're here now," Imogen said, eager to play peacemaker. "And we're so happy that you are."

Her husband grunted as he scooped mashed potatoes onto his plate.

Charlotte picked up her glass of wine, sipped.

"I hope Allison can make it for Christmas this year, too," her mom said. "It would be nice to have all of our girls home."

"They won't all be home," Thaddeus pointed out. "Your youngest daughter is still at that hotel."

"The Heights is a beautiful hotel," Charlotte felt compelled to point out.

"Do you prefer it to this house, too?" her father asked. "Is that why you've been spending so much time there?"

"I've been spending time there because that's where Eloise and Merry are."

"Maybe they'd come here to visit if you were here."

Charlotte poured more wine into her glass.

Conversation ceased for the next several minutes as everyone focused on the food on their plates.

"Juliana Meyer said that she saw you at Pastabilities last night when she was picking up a takeout order," Imogen said, breaking the silence that had fallen around the table.

"I didn't see her," Charlotte replied, though she wasn't sure she would have recognized her mother's friend after so many years.

"Who were you having dinner with?" Thaddeus wanted to know.

"Billy Abernathy."

"What are you doing hanging around with him?" her father demanded.

Charlotte sighed. "As you already noted, we were having dinner."

"Maybe you've forgotten how people in this town talk, but they do, and the last thing we need is for you to stir up chatter about the wedding that you walked out on."

"It was twenty years ago," Charlotte reminded him. "I suspect most people have forgotten."

"Well, they likely haven't forgotten that the man's recently divorced. You don't need to be getting tangled up in that kind of messiness."

"Maybe a man who's recently divorced needs a friend," she countered, as Imogen quietly got up from the table.

"You never did listen to reason," Thaddeus grumbled.

"Why is it when one of my brothers challenges something you say, they're applauded for demonstrating that they've got their own thoughts and opinions, but when it's me or one of my sisters, we don't listen to reason?"

Thaddeus pounded his fist on the table, making the dishes clatter. "Because none of you girls listens to reason."

"Look what Lina made," Imogen said, returning to the table with a bowl of trifle.

Charlotte took another sip of her wine. "Thanks, Mom. But I don't want any dessert tonight."

"But…it's your favorite."

Except that it wasn't.

She liked trifle well enough, but cheesecake was her favorite.

But even if her mom had come in with an entire cheesecake, Charlotte wouldn't have been able to stay there a single minute longer.

She set her glass down and pushed away from the table. "Thank you for dinner."

And then she retreated to her room.

Billy had just returned home after dinner with his parents when his phone buzzed. He glanced at the screen, his interest piquing when he saw that the message was from Charlotte.

Are you busy?

He immediately replied:

Not at all. What's up?

I need to get out of this house. Could we meet for a drink somewhere?

"This house" clearly meant Thaddeus and Imogen's mansion on the Triple T.

He considered the options. There was The Association, of course, though the exclusive club was bound to be filled with people who knew both Thaddeus Taylor and Asa Abernathy—many of whom had likely been guests at the wedding-that-never-happened. And he wasn't sure either he or Charlotte wanted to deal with the questions that might be raised by their appearance there together. Doug's wasn't a much better option, and it would be a fair trek into town for both of them. Wild Willa's was closer, but it tended to be packed on weekends, making conversation difficult.

Why don't I pick you up?

I'll meet you at the bottom of the driveway.

It was what she'd done countless times in the past, when she'd snuck out of the house to be with him.

Not that Thaddeus had disapproved of their relationship, but he'd liked to be in control. To say "no" when she asked if she could go out, just because he was the dad and he said so.

When Jill was born, Billy promised himself that he'd never do the same thing to his own daughter. He'd also vowed to make sure it was a sheer drop to the ground from her second-story bedroom so that she couldn't sneak out her window as he knew Charlotte had frequently done.

Twenty minutes?

Perfect.

He pulled up at the end of the driveway just as she reached the same spot. She opened the passenger side door and hopped into the cab of his truck, laughing as she pulled the door shut.

"I'm having the strangest feeling of déjà vu."

"You know you'll be grounded if he realizes you snuck out," Billy warned, in an echo of the words he'd said to her countless times before.

"Totally worth it," she said, giving him her usual reply.

"Did you have a fight with your dad?" he asked, his tone serious now.

"How'd you guess?"

"The two of you were in the same room together."

She laughed at that, though the sound was without humor. "Isn't that the truth?"

"What was it about this time?"

"He just can't trust me to make my own decisions. No," she said, immediately correcting herself. "It's not just me. He treats Allison and Eloise the same way."

"Might be why all of you left Bronco as soon as the opportunity presented itself."

"Funny how everyone else can see that except him."

He turned onto the road leading to the Bonnie B.

"Where are we going?"

"You said you wanted a drink."

"It wasn't code for sex," she told him.

"I promise, my mind did *not* go there."

"And isn't that all the proof we need that we're not seventeen anymore?" she mused.

"If you're not comfortable at my place, we could head over to The Associ—"

"God, no," she said, cutting him off. "And your place is fine. Great, actually."

"I should probably warn you that your drink options will be limited."

"Beggars can't be choosers," she said, as he pulled into the driveway beside a two-story farmhouse of stone and brick with a covered porch that appeared to wrap around all sides.

Clearly he wasn't a beggar, Charlotte mused, as it was apparent no expense had been spared in the construction of the gorgeous home. It was the type of house they'd talked about building one day—there was just one thing missing.

"You need a porch swing," she told him, when he opened the passenger side door for her.

"I've got one," he said, offering a hand to help her out of the truck. "But it goes into storage in the barn in the winter."

"That makes sense," she noted. "It's not as if you'd want to sit out on a night like tonight."

"Actually, this is a perfect night for sitting out under the stars," he said. "Just look at them."

She tipped her head back to peer up at the sky. He was right—the view was absolutely spectacular, like a thousand brilliant diamonds scattered on black velvet. "Very nice—except that it's hard to see through my breath fogging the air."

Chuckling, he reached past her to twist the knob and open the front door of dark wood with textured glass inserts.

She entered the foyer ahead of him, removing her coat and boots as he did the same.

"Tell me about these limited drink options," she said.

"I've got some Coors Light in the fridge and a bottle of Big Horn Bourbon Whiskey in the cupboard."

"Hmm... I think I'll go for the whiskey," she decided.

"Must have been some fight," he noted.

"It wasn't really." She followed him down the hall and into the living room, travertine tile giving way to luxurious hardwood. The room was furnished with a wide sofa and several oversize chairs covered in suede fabric with a trio of wood-and-glass tables. One wall was dominated by an enormous television flanked by tall windows, another boasted a stunning floor-to-ceiling fireplace.

Billy opened one of the glass-fronted bookcases that spanned the length of the third wall, then slid a boxed set of books aside to retrieve the bottle of whiskey stashed behind it.

"You hide your alcohol behind *The Complete History of Middle Earth*?"

"I have a seventeen-year-old who isn't much of a reader," he explained. "No way would he go near Tolkien."

"Clever."

He uncapped the bottle and poured a generous splash into each of two glasses.

"Cheers," she said, tapping her glass against his before lifting it to her lips.

"You were telling me about the fight with your dad," he reminded her.

"There's not much to tell. And maybe that's why I'm so frustrated—it was just same old, same old. He never changes."

She swallowed another mouthful of whiskey, then sighed. "This was probably a bad idea."

"The whiskey?"

She shook her head. "Texting you."

"Do you want me to take you home?"

"No… Yes." She tossed back the rest of her drink. "Maybe."

"Well, that clears things up."

"I'm only going to be in town until the New Year."

"You mentioned that."

He held the bottle over her glass—a silent question. She hesitated, then nodded.

He poured her another drink.

"And I get why you might not want to get involved," she said, picking up the thread of conversation again. "But it occurred to me that if I'm only here for another couple of weeks, maybe we shouldn't waste any time."

He was starting to think he knew where she was going with this, but he was afraid to get his hopes up, in case it turned out that he was wrong.

She set her glass down on the table and moved toward him, and those tentative hopes lifted despite his internal warnings.

"You've barely touched your whiskey," she noted.

"Having you here is more intoxicating than alcohol."

She smiled and took another step closer. "Do you think so?"

Before he could respond to that, she'd lifted her hands to his shoulders and rose up on her toes to brush her lips against his. It was a casual kiss, but the way his body immediately responded to the light touch of her mouth was anything but casual.

As if of their own volition, his arms went around her, drawing her closer. Close enough that her breasts grazed his chest, causing all of the blood in his head to migrate south. He kissed her back, not so casual. Her lips parted willingly, allowing him to deepen the kiss. Their tongues dallied and danced together, an intimate advance and retreat that mimicked the rhythm of lovemaking and made him suddenly, achingly aware that it had been a very long time since he'd made love with a woman. And much, much too long since he'd had the pleasure of making love with *this* woman.

He eased his mouth from hers. "Please tell me this isn't some kind of rebellion against your father?"

"I promise you, my father is the furthest thing from my mind right now."

"So what is this about?" he asked, needing to be clear.

"It's about the fact that I've never wanted anyone the way I want you. And that I haven't been able to think about anything but how much I want you since that kiss last night."

"I thought we were blaming that kiss on the mistletoe."

"Is there any mistletoe here?"

"No." Not even a swag of garland or snowman decoration, she realized, though there was a pile of red-and-green boxes in the corner that she suspected held his Christmas decorations. "When are you going to get ready for the holidays?"

"Is that really what you want to talk about now?"

She closed her eyes on a sigh as his hands slid under her sweater to cup her breasts. "No."

He drew his hands away. "No?"

She grabbed his hands and put them back on her breasts. "No I don't want to talk about your lack of Christmas decorations," she clarified. "In fact, I don't want to talk at all. But I do want you to touch me."

"Good. Because I want to touch you."

And he spent the next several minutes doing just that, listening to her soft sighs and throaty moans as he thoroughly relearned every dip and curve of her body.

"Are we crazy for doing this?" she asked breathlessly.

"We're not talking," he reminded her.

"If you don't want me to talk, you should kiss me," she said.

So he did.

And while he was kissing her, he cupped her bottom and lifted her off the floor. She wrapped her legs around his waist, anchoring herself against him, and he carried her that way to his bedroom.

"I do have to say one thing," he noted, pausing inside the doorway.

"What's that?"

"It's going to be a nice change to make love with you in a real bed rather than the bed of my truck."

"I have very fond memories of that truck," she assured him.

"Let's see if I can create fond memories for you here," he said, and tumbled with her onto the mattress.

Chapter Eleven

He started by stripping away her sweater and jeans, leaving her clad in a pale blue cotton bra and hip-hugger panties. There was nothing special about her underwear—except for the woman wearing them. And to Billy, Charlotte in cotton was sexier than any lingerie model in silk or lace.

She'd managed to undo only half the buttons that ran down the front of his shirt before he yanked the garment over his head and tossed it aside. Then her hands were on him, her fingertips tracing the ridges of his abdomen, making his muscles tense and quiver.

He slid a hand behind her back, making quick work of the clasp before whisking her bra away, baring her breasts. He captured them in his hands, his thumbs circling her nipples, causing them to draw into tight points that begged for closer attention. He gave them that attention, with his hands and his mouth, making her pant and writhe.

Though he was still half-dressed, she parted her legs to fit him between them, lifting her hips to rub against his arousal. Despite the layers of denim and cotton that separated them, the glorious friction was almost more than he could bear. He pulled away from her to shed the rest of his clothes, then knelt on the mattress again, spreading her knees wide and lowering his head to nuzzle her through the soft cotton panties. A moan sounded low in her throat and her hips instinctively lifted off the bed, giving him better access to the center of her pleasure. He licked and sucked through the cotton, making the fabric wet both inside and out, using her sighs and moans as his guide in leading her toward the ultimate pinnacle of pleasure.

"Billy…please. I need…"

"Tell me what you need," he said.

"You. Inside me."

He dispensed with her damp panties and rose over her, eager to give her what she wanted. What they both wanted. Then drew back and swore.

She braced herself on her elbows. "What's wrong?"

"I don't have— Wait a minute."

He rolled off the bed and hurried down the hall.

She was smiling when he returned. "You just pilfered a box of condoms from the boys' bathroom, didn't you?"

"I'll replace it before they get back."

"I'm just grateful there was a box to be pilfered," she said, taking the square packet from his hand.

She opened it carefully and unrolled the latex over

his erection, teasingly stroking the length of him, then gliding her fingers up again.

He lowered his head to kiss her, easing her back down on the bed as he deepened the kiss. She drew up her knees, opening for him. It was all the invitation he needed. In one slow, deep thrust, he buried himself inside her. She gasped with pleasure, tilting her hips to take him even deeper. He captured her hands and linked their fingers together, so they were joined in every possible way.

As their bodies moved in sync, their hearts beat in tandem, finding a rhythm that was somehow both achingly familiar and surprisingly new and that carried them into the abyss of pleasure together.

Charlotte fell asleep with her head on Billy's chest, listening to the steady rhythm of his heart beating.

She woke up a few hours later and squinted at the clock on his bedside table.

2:47.

She hated to wake him, but she needed to get back to her parents' house and she could hardly walk there from here.

"Billy?" She put a hand on his shoulder and shook it gently.

He immediately sat up in the bed. "What's wrong?"

"Nothing's wrong."

"Sorry." He scrubbed his hands over his face. "Whenever one of the kids woke me up in the night, there was always something wrong."

"I haven't spent much time with you and your kids, but from what I've seen, you are a really great dad."

"Like you said, you haven't spent much time with me and my kids."

"They're good kids," she noted. "That says a lot right there."

"Most of the credit for that belongs to their mother."

"And yet, you jolted awake thinking that one of them needed something."

"Well, I was the go-to when Jill thought there might be monsters under her bed," he acknowledged.

"And how did you handle that?"

"Monster spray, of course."

She smiled, because it was all too easy to picture him crouched beside his young daughter's bed, spraying to keep the monsters away. All too easy to imagine that he would have been the same kind of amazing father to the child they'd almost had together.

And then, to her complete mortification, Charlotte began to cry.

"I have tears-be-gone spray, too," he said. "Do you want me to get it?"

She managed to smile even while she was crying. "I always knew you'd be an awesome dad. But I thought you'd be an awesome dad to *our* kids."

"Me, too," he admitted.

"I know it's my fault it never happened. When I lost our baby, I grieved, because I loved her as soon as I learned of her existence. But at the same time, I was relieved not to be pregnant, because I wasn't ready to be a mother."

"I was relieved, too," he confided. "I loved you and wanted to marry you, but I wasn't quite so eager to tackle parenthood."

She nodded, grateful for his admission. "And I believed that when the time was right, when I was ready, I would get to be a mom. But the time never seemed to be right—or maybe I've just never been with anyone that I wanted to have a family with—and now I can't help but wonder if I'll ever have a child of my own."

"I'm sorry, Charlotte."

She dashed away the tears. "I'm the one who should be apologizing. I didn't plan to have a meltdown."

"We're friends," he reminded her. "If you can't melt down in front of your friends, who can you melt down in front of?"

And there it was—the reminder of what they were and weren't to one another. Never mind that they'd just had earth-shaking sex, Billy was firmly keeping her in the friend zone.

She nodded. "Well, I need a ride home, friend."

"You don't want to stay for breakfast?"

"I'd love to stay for breakfast, but I don't want to deal with the questions I'll have to answer if I'm not home in the morning."

"We could have breakfast now," he said.

"It's three o'clock in the morning."

"Keyword—*morning.*"

"I am not eating breakfast at three a.m.," she said.

"Okay." He captured her hand and yanked her back down onto the bed. "I can keep you busy for another half an hour."

And he did.

And it was amazing.

And then he fried up bacon and scrambled eggs while she toasted bread.

Billy liked seeing Charlotte there, in his home, her hair tousled around her face, a look of sleepy satisfaction on her face. And it made him feel good to know that he was responsible for that look.

"What are you thinking?" she asked him.

"I was thinking that if we'd done this Friday night, we could have done it again Saturday, but my kids are going to be home tonight, so there's no chance of an encore performance."

"I understand that they're your priority—as they should be."

"But they're going to be at their mom's again on Wednesday for dinner."

"Is that an invitation for me to come for…dinner on Wednesday?"

He smiled. "I could make something for us to eat."

"I like the sound of that," she said, smiling back at him. "But now, I really need to get home."

So he took her to the Triple T—and bravely pulled into the driveway to deliver her to the front door.

"You were supposed to drop me off at the bottom of the driveway," she admonished.

"You're a grown woman," he reminded her. "I don't think you really need to worry about your father grounding you."

"I'm more worried about being questioned than grounded. But either way, tonight was totally worth whatever fallout might happen." Then she leaned across the center console to kiss him goodbye. "What time should I come by for dinner on Wednesday?"

"Does five o'clock work?"

"I'll see you at five o'clock," she confirmed.

He drove away, already looking forward to it.

"I'm sorry for storming out last night," Charlotte said to her mom, when she walked into the dining room for a much-needed cup of coffee Sunday morning.

"You don't have to apologize to me," Imogen assured her. "I can't tell you how many times I've been tempted to do the same thing."

"How do you put up with it?" Charlotte wondered, carrying her mug to the table and taking a seat across from her mother.

"Your father might not be the easiest man to live with, but he's my husband and the father of my children and I love him."

Charlotte didn't dare question her mother's assertion—or ask why. Whatever had brought her parents together—and kept them together—was a mystery to her and one that she didn't particularly want to unravel.

"And he's not wrong to be concerned about you spending time with Billy," Imogen said gently.

"Are you worried about the gossip, too?"

"No," her mom denied. "I'm worried about your heart. Because I know that you didn't run out of your own wedding because you didn't love him."

"I think maybe I loved him too much," she admitted.

"And that scared you."

"That—and the prospect of becoming a wife only days after my high school graduation."

"I blamed myself," her mom finally said. "For not being more aware of what was going on between you. For not making sure you were protected."

"It wasn't your fault," Charlotte assured her. "We'd both taken the mandatory sex ed classes—we knew how babies were made and what precautions to take."

"But you were young and in love and careless."

"But we started out as friends," she reminded her mom. "And that's why it's been good to spend time with him now. To reconnect after so many years and discover that we can be friends again."

"How much time have you been spending with him?"

"Well, I saw him at the career fair. And then our paths crossed at Sadie's Holiday House, and we went for coffee. Then I saw him at the holiday concert at the high school. And Friday night we had dinner."

She thought it best not to mention that she'd snuck out to see him the night before—and ended up in his bed.

Especially as Imogen looked troubled enough without that additional information.

"I promise that I'm not going to fall in love with him again," she told her mother.

"I can't pretend to find that reassuring, because I know only too well that we can't control how or when— or with whom—we fall in love."

"Then maybe you'll be reassured by the fact that I'm heading to Florida after the New Year."

"I think I'd rather you fell in love with Billy Abernathy again—especially if it meant you'd move back to Bronco."

"If I ever fall in love again, I hope I won't have to choose between a relationship and my career, which is what would happen if I fell in love with someone in Montana."

"That would be a tough choice," her mom acknowledged. "Though I'd argue that love—true love—is worth any sacrifice.

"And now—" she pushed away from the table "—I should make sure that Lina's got the bacon started, because Thaddeus is going to be up soon and looking for his breakfast."

"And I should be heading out," Charlotte said, eager to avoid another confrontation with her father. Because it seemed as if there was always a confrontation with her father.

"Where are you going this early on a Sunday morning?"

"I've got some errands to run."

"None of the shops are going to be open yet," Imogen warned.

Charlotte kissed her cheek. "I'll see you later."

It didn't take her long to realize that her mother was right. None of the shops was open and there really wasn't anything else to do on a Sunday morning. And so, with nowhere else to go, she found herself driving to Bronco Heights Community Church.

The church where she'd left Billy—and their dreams—behind.

She'd dressed out of habit in jeans and a sweater that

morning—not what her mother would consider appropriate attire for a place of worship, but she didn't think God judged people on the basis of what they wore on Sundays or any other day of the week.

To Charlotte, nature was evidence of God's existence, but she had no trouble understanding how others might see Him in soaring ceilings and stained glass windows and find comfort in the scent of lemon polish or lingering notes of smoky incense. And when she slid into a vacant pew near the back of the church, she experienced a welcome feeling of peacefulness, almost like what she'd found the night before in Billy's arms.

Perhaps that wasn't something she should be thinking about while she was in church, but she couldn't seem to help herself. Since their first encounter at the high school career fair, he'd been on her mind almost constantly, tempting her thoughts to wander down the dangerous path of *what if.* And though she knew there was no way to go back and change the past, she suddenly found herself re-evaluating what she wanted for her future.

Though the minister's sermon didn't provide her with any immediate answers, she enjoyed the service. And after leaving the church, she decided to grab a coffee at Bronco Java and Juice.

She paid for her drink and glanced around, looking for a vacant seat. She found something even better—a familiar face—and moved toward the table by the window.

"Sadie?"

Her new friend glanced up, a smile curving her lips.

"Charlotte Taylor. What a nice surprise you are on this cold winter morning."

"And you," Charlotte agreed.

"Please, sit," Sadie said, gesturing to the trio of empty chairs around the table.

Charlotte did so. "What brings you to this part of town so early on a Sunday?"

"A meeting with Father Bruce before church. Which I'm sure he scheduled at that time so that Sullivan and I would stay for the service, and since he's marrying us in eight days, it would have looked bad to skip out— though Sullivan did, claiming there was a problem with one of the windmills at the Flying A."

"And you wished you could have skipped out with him," Charlotte guessed.

"It's just a really busy time of year. For everyone, I know," the shopkeeper acknowledged. "But in addition to the usual countdown to Christmas chaos at Holiday House, I'm worried about wedding details potentially falling through the cracks."

"Wait a minute." Charlotte held up a hand. "You just said that you're getting married in eight days."

Sadie nodded.

"And Christmas is in eight days."

Another nod.

"You're getting married *on Christmas*?"

"We are," the other woman confirmed. "And I've had no shortage of people tell me that we're crazy for doing so. But December 25 is already my favorite day of the year, and marrying the man I know I'll love forever will only make it more so."

"A bride's wedding day should be the happiest day of her life," Charlotte noted, because no shortage of people had said exactly that to her.

"Plus, Sullivan isn't likely to ever forget our anniversary."

Charlotte had to laugh. "Well, crazy or not, I think the important thing is to have the wedding that *you* want. And I imagine your Christmas wedding will be absolutely beautiful."

"Instead of imagining it, you should come and see for yourself," Sadie told her.

"Oh, no. I'm not going to crash your wedding," she protested.

"It's not crashing if you're invited."

"Are you really inviting me?"

"Of course," her new friend confirmed.

Warmth suffused her cheeks in response to the kindness of her new friend's offer. "In that case, I wouldn't miss it," Charlotte promised.

"Great." Sadie glanced at her watch. "But right now, I need to be at Holiday House."

Charlotte gave her new friend a quick hug and promised to see her at her Christmas wedding—if not before.

She'd just settled back into her seat when Jill Abernathy walked in. Charlotte's heart immediately skipped a beat—because she assumed the girl's dad would be close behind. Instead, she saw that Jill was with a woman who could only be her mother.

Billy's ex-wife was stunningly beautiful, with blunt-cut shoulder-length auburn hair and blue eyes. She was of average height and slender build, wearing a long coat and high-heeled boots with a designer bag over her shoulder.

Jill was talking animatedly to her mom, obviously basking in the woman's attention, as they waited their turn at the counter.

Which made Charlotte wonder how this woman—or any woman—could leave her family. Her partner, sure. There were countless reasons that a romantic relationship might fall apart. But Charlotte felt confident that if she was ever blessed with children, there was nothing in the world that could compel her to leave them.

Mom and daughter received their order and turned to look for a table, which was when Jill spotted Charlotte and walked over.

A smile spread across her face. "Miss Taylor, hi."

"Hello, Jill."

The other woman put out a hand. "I'm Jill's mom, Jane Sinclair."

"Charlotte Taylor." She shook the proffered hand. "It's nice to meet you."

"Can we sit with you?" Jill asked.

"Of course," she said, because even if there were other empty tables in the café (and there were), it was hardly a request she could refuse without appearing incredibly rude. And truthfully, she was a little bit curious about the woman who'd been Billy's wife for eighteen years.

"Thank you," Jane said, lowering herself into the seat across from Charlotte, on the other side of her daughter.

"Mmm, that looks good," Charlotte said, eyeing Jill's pastry.

"Do you want a piece?" the girl immediately offered.

"No, thanks. It seems like everywhere I go, there are Christmas treats and if I continue to indulge, I won't fit into my wetsuit when I get back to the Bahamas."

"Is that where you live?" Jane asked.

"It's where I work," Charlotte clarified.

"Miss Taylor's the marine biologist I was telling you about," Jill told her mom.

"Ah, yes. My daughter is quite fascinated by your work with dolphins," Jane said to Charlotte.

"It's fascinating work," she agreed.

For the next few minutes, Jill carried the conversation while the adults sipped their respective beverages and responded as required.

"There's Kelli and Sam," Jill said, pushing away from the table. "I'm going to go say hi."

And then she was gone, leaving Charlotte and Jane alone at the table.

"In case you were wondering," Jane said, when her daughter was out of earshot, "I'm well aware that you're more than a marine biologist and an old friend of my ex-husband."

"What is it that you think you know?" Charlotte asked, certain there wasn't any way the other woman could know that she'd spent the night—or at least several fabulous hours—in her ex-husband's bed.

"I know that you were Billy's high school sweetheart," Jane said, responding to her question. "The one who got away—literally—by leaving him at the altar."

"Apparently my five minutes of fame—or infamy—hasn't been forgotten, even twenty years later."

"You broke his heart."

"So did you," Charlotte noted.

But Jane shook her head. "I might have wounded his pride, but I know I didn't break his heart because he never gave it to me. Because he never got over you."

An unexpected warmth filled Charlotte's chest as she considered the possibility that the feelings she still had for Billy might be reciprocated.

But even if it was true—did it matter? Because his life was in Bronco and her time here was limited.

Jane glanced across the room to ensure that her daughter was still busy chatting with her friends before she continued. "And although I know I bear most of the responsibility for the break-up of my family, I want them to be happy. Not just my kids, but Billy, too."

She shifted her gaze to meet Charlotte's then. "You might be the one person who can make him happy. But I also worry that you could break his heart again."

"I don't think you don't need to worry about Billy," Charlotte told her.

The other woman shrugged. "We were married for more than eighteen years and old habits die hard."

She acknowledged the point with a nod.

"And while I know your relationship with Billy isn't any of my business—"

"It's not," Charlotte interjected to agree.

"I hope you care enough about him not to lead him on if you're only planning to leave again," his ex-wife continued, ignoring the interruption.

"Billy knows what my plans are."

"Maybe in his head," Jane acknowledged. "But the heart is a different matter."

It was a truth that Charlotte knew only too well.

Billy hadn't managed to get much sleep the night before, but instead of feeling tired Sunday morning as he and his brothers did their chores on the Bonnie B, he felt oddly energized.

"Someone's in a good mood today," Theo remarked.

Billy cut the twine on the bale of hay. "What are you talking about?"

"You were whistling."

"No, I wasn't." The denial was automatic, because he knew he wasn't in the habit of whistling while he worked.

"Actually, you were," Jace confirmed, forcing Billy to acknowledge that he likely had been.

"Well, why wouldn't I be in a good mood?" he said with a shrug. "The sky's blue and the sun's shining."

Theo's eyes narrowed as he gave his elder brother an assessing look. "You spent the night with a woman."

Billy concentrated on spreading the feed over the ground.

"Please tell me it wasn't Jane," Theo implored.

"I'm not telling you anything," Billy said. "Except that no, it definitely wasn't Jane."

"That's a relief," Jace said.

Billy glanced up at the sky, hoping to shift the topic of conversation. "The forecast is calling for snow, but I don't see it."

"It wouldn't be the first time the weatherman was wrong," Jace noted.

"True," he agreed.

"Charlotte?" Theo guessed.

"What?"

"Were you with Charlotte last night?" his brother pressed, proving that Billy's efforts to shift the conversation had been futile.

"Which part of 'not telling you anything' didn't you understand?"

"It was Charlotte," Theo decided.

"How do you know?" Jace wondered aloud.

"Because Billy's not the type to pick up a random woman in a bar. Plus, I was at Doug's last night and he wasn't."

"There are other bars in town," Billy pointed out to his brothers.

"You're not going to pick up a woman at The Association—because it's pretty much a guarantee that she'd be some member's sister or daughter or wife."

Billy couldn't deny there was some truth in that.

"Again, there are other bars in town," he said instead.

"Yeah, but none that you're likely to hang out in," Theo noted.

"Glad to know I'm so predictable."

"It's probably more that you really haven't had a chance to have a life," Jace said. "You were married for eighteen years and are only recently divorced—which is why it's good that you hooked up last night. You needed to be with someone else, so that now you won't be moping around thinking 'the last woman I had sex with was my wife.'"

"Have you been watching Dr. Phil in your spare time?"

"Mock me all you want—you know I'm right."

"What I want is to get this feed out for the cows."

"What's your rush?" Theo asked. "You got a hot date this afternoon?"

"I promised the kids that we'd go out to get a tree when they got home from their mom's."

"You don't have a tree yet?" Jace asked. "What are you waiting for—Christmas?"

Theo laughed as if their brother's lame joke was the funniest thing he'd ever heard.

Billy ignored them both and focused on finishing his chores.

At two o'clock, Jane brought the kids home—and Jill presented Billy with a container full of cookies she and her mom had baked. When everyone was bundled up in their outdoor gear, they trudged through the snow to the woods to select a Christmas tree.

Apparently Billy's good mood lingered, because Branson turned and looked at him, a quizzical expression on his face.

"What?" he asked.

"You're whistling."

This time, he didn't bother to deny it. "So?"

Branson shrugged. "I just haven't heard you whistle in a long time."

"I guess Christmas tree hunting puts me in a good mood."

"Then maybe we should cut down a Christmas tree every day," Jill said.

"Ha ha," Billy replied.

"We'd run out of trees pretty quickly if we did," Nicky pointed out. "But it might be worth it."

"Have I been so difficult to live with?" Billy wondered aloud.

"Not difficult," Branson said, "but…"

"Not happy," Jill finished for her brother.

"I'm sorry," he said. "I thought I was doing a better job at hiding my feelings."

"You don't need to apologize," Branson told him. "None of us has been too happy these last few months."

"Well, let's try to change that—starting today," Billy suggested.

Because he did want this to be an enjoyable outing for them, though he'd worried that they'd compare this year with last. This year, it was only the four of them; last year, they'd been a family of five.

But in all honesty, Billy thought this year was better.

Of course, the kids hadn't known that their parents' relationship had been incredibly strained the previous year. At least, he hoped they hadn't known. He and Jane had agreed to keep things as normal as possible, even after she'd told him she was thinking of moving out of the house.

She hadn't told him that moving out of their house meant moving in with her boyfriend—because she hadn't yet told him that there was a boyfriend.

He'd been such a fool.

He had no idea when she'd started sleeping with

Henri—or if she'd still been sleeping with Billy at the same time. He doubted it, as their sex life had dwindled to almost nothing in recent years. But he hadn't wanted to ask, so he'd made a point of going to see his doctor and having some tests done—just to be safe. Thankfully all the results were negative, though his relief was tempered by the humiliation of having to ask for the tests in the first place.

He pushed those unhappy memories out of his mind to focus on making new, happier memories with his kids now. Like finding the perfect Christmas tree.

"Mom's got a fake tree," Jill said, as Billy and Branson wrestled into the stand the fir they'd cut down. "It's about twelve feet tall and decorated in silver and gold."

"Sounds fancy," he said.

"I guess it looks nice," she allowed.

"It looks weird," Nicky said. "It's got this fake snow stuff on the branches—as if a tree in the house would ever have snow on its branches."

"A puddle on the floor from melted snow would be more realistic," Branson chimed in.

"I just don't get why anyone would want a plastic tree," Nicky said.

"Mom said it's because Henri's allergic to real trees," Jill said.

"Is that even a thing?" Nicky asked.

Billy shrugged. "How would I know?"

"Anyway," Jill said, sounding unhappy as she threaded a hanger onto an ornament, "Mom didn't even wait for us to help decorate the fake tree."

"If there are specific things you want to do with your mom, you need to tell her," Billy advised in a gentle tone.

"We didn't need to tell you," she pointed out. "We've been gone since Friday, but we didn't come home to find that you'd gotten a tree without us."

"Well, of course, I wouldn't get a tree without you," he said.

"Why not?"

"Because it's a family tradition to pick out our tree together."

"Exactly," she said smugly.

While Branson, Nicky and Jill finished decorating the tree, Billy put water on the stove to boil and defrosted a container of meat sauce for a quick and easy pasta dinner. After they'd eaten and tidied up the kitchen, they returned to the living room to watch a holiday movie—another family tradition.

When the kids were younger, they'd usually chosen an animated feature—*Frosty the Snowman, A Charlie Brown Christmas* and *How the Grinch Stole Christmas* being perennial favorites. As they got older, they moved on to full-length movies. This year, Jill had voted for *Elf,* Nicky wanted *A Christmas Story*, and Branson campaigned for *Die Hard*. So Billy wrote each title on a slip of paper, put it in a hat and pulled out a winner. Then they settled in front of the television with freshly popped corn, the room dark except for the picture on the screen and the multicolored lights on the Christmas tree.

Branson claimed the armchair and Nicky sank into his beanbag chair, but Jill snuggled up against her dad on the sofa. And as an adult Ralphie began to narrate his story, Billy decided that maybe this Christmas wasn't going to be so bad, after all.

Still, he couldn't help thinking that having Charlotte around would make it even better.

Chapter Twelve

Monday morning, Charlotte was happy to get a text message from her sister asking her to stop by the hotel. Apparently Dante was running errands and Eloise didn't want to sit around twiddling her thumbs. Instead, they bundled up the baby and took her out for a walk.

"How did I think I was going to survive Montana in December without thermal underwear?" Charlotte grumbled as she pulled the collar of her coat around her neck.

"Is it too cold out here for you?" Eloise asked.

"If Merry can handle it, I should be able to," she said bravely.

"Merry is covered from head to toe in about four layers."

"I'll be okay," Charlotte said. "But maybe we could walk a little faster."

Her sister obligingly picked up the pace.

"How are the folks?"

"Mom's good. Dad makes me crazy."

"So the usual," Eloise said, not really joking.

"The usual," Charlotte agreed.

"You don't have to stay with them, you know. I'd be happy to have you come back to the hotel and stay with us," Eloise said, not for the first time.

"I appreciate the offer, but your relationship with Dante is still new. I don't want to cramp your style."

"Our relationship is so new, we don't yet have a style," her sister said. "Not to mention that I gave birth just over two weeks ago, so we're literally sleeping together— nothing more than that. And only when Merry lets us sleep."

"And that's another reason for me to stay at the ranch," Charlotte said. "Dad might be a blowhard, but at least he sleeps through the night."

Eloise laughed at that.

"But I do have a confession to make," Charlotte told her sister.

"What's that?"

"Dad got me so worked up Saturday night that I snuck out of the house, like I used to do when I was a teenager."

"But you're not a teenager, so why did you feel the need to sneak?"

She shrugged. "Maybe I was feeling nostalgic for my younger days."

"Where'd you go?"

"To Billy's."

Eloise raised her eyebrows. "Were his kids home?"

Charlotte shook her head. "No, they were with their mom this weekend."

"So you went to Billy's empty house?"

Now she nodded.

"And then?" her sister prompted.

"We had a drink together."

"And then?" Eloise said again.

"We had sex."

Her sister grinned. "Good for you."

"Is it?" Charlotte wondered.

"Wasn't it?"

She couldn't hold back the smile that curved her lips. "Okay, yes. It was good. In fact, it was phenomenal. But it was an impulse and I didn't really think about the repercussions."

"Repercussions?" Eloise's jaw dropped. "Do you think… Could you be pregnant?"

"No," she responded quickly, ignoring the tug on her heart. "Not those kinds of repercussions. The emotional kind."

"Oh." Her sister almost sounded disappointed. "It would have been kind of cool for Merry to have a cousin close in age."

"Close in age but living far away."

"Yeah. I guess I forgot that part for a minute."

"And anyway, we took the usual precautions."

"So…are you guys together now? Or was this a one-night thing?"

"Well, he invited me to come over for dinner on Wednesday—when the kids are with their mom again—so I'm hoping it's more than a one-night thing."

"Does he know you're planning to leave after the New Year?"

"Yes, he knows."

"Any chance he might change your mind?" Eloise asked hopefully.

"He hasn't given any indication of wanting to change my mind," Charlotte said.

"But if he did?"

She didn't know how to answer that question—or even if she wanted to—so she was grateful when Kendra's Cupcakes came into sight.

"How does hot chocolate sound?" she asked her sister instead.

"Like music to my ears," Eloise said, just as Charlotte's phone pinged.

She pulled it out of her pocket, frowning at the unfamiliar number displayed on the screen.

"Do you need to get that?"

She nodded. "It could be news about the grant."

"Okay. I'll meet you inside."

As Eloise maneuvered Merry's all-weather stroller into the bakery, Charlotte swiped to connect the call.

"Hello?"

"Is this Charlotte Taylor?"

"Yes," she said cautiously.

"My name is Sean McCaffrey. I'm calling on behalf of the Seaway Group in Wonderstone Ridge."

Charlotte knew of the town that was about thirty minutes north of Bronco, of course, but she'd never heard of the Seaway Group and had no idea why they might be reaching out to her. "How can I help you, Mr. Mc-Caffrey?"

"Sean, please," he said. "And I'm glad you asked…"

Five minutes later, when Charlotte joined her sister inside, she gratefully accepted the mug of hot chocolate with whipped cream and chocolate drizzle that Eloise pushed across the table to her.

"We were going to share a gingerbread cookie, too, but you were gone too long and all that's left now are crumbs."

"Was it a good cookie?"

"It was a *great* cookie." Eloise sipped her hot chocolate. "Was the call about your grant?"

She shook her head. "Did you know there's an aquarium and marine discovery center being built in Wonderstone Ridge?"

"I did hear something about that," her sister said. "I think it's still under construction, but they're hoping for a late spring or early summer opening. Wait a minute—" Her eyes went wide. "Is that who called you? Did they offer you a job?"

"Not quite," Charlotte said. "But they want to meet with me, to discuss the possibility. Apparently a former supervisor of mine gave them my name as a potential head of the education department."

"That's so exciting!" Eloise looked at her sister's stunned face. "Isn't it?"

"I'm trying not to think too far ahead," Charlotte admitted. "I mean, it would be a big change, but it also has the potential to be a great opportunity."

"You could move back home."

She could move back home…but did she want to?

Over the years, she hadn't let herself think too much about what she might be missing out on in Montana because she'd been busy with her work. She definitely hadn't let herself think about how much she missed her family. Sure, she sometimes joined holiday gatherings via Skype or Zoom, but it wasn't the same as being there.

And sometimes she was glad it wasn't the same as being there.

But the truth was, almost constant arguments with her father notwithstanding, she missed her family when she was away from them. She loved her job and the people she worked with—and she knew that working at a marine discovery center wouldn't be as exciting as working in the field and observing dolphins in their natural habitat. But it was important work. Education was a vital aspect of conservation.

And to be perfectly honest, working with young graduates fresh out of college, she was starting to feel as if she was ready for a change.

Or maybe she just really wanted an excuse to stay in Bronco—especially now that she and Billy had reconnected.

"I could move back home," she agreed cautiously.

"Speaking from experience, I understand it's a big decision. Huge," Eloise said. "But for what it's worth, I'd love to be able to see you more regularly. And Merry would love to spend more time with her aunt."

"Really? You're using your baby as incentive?"

Her sister grinned. "Whatever works."

"Well, the possibility of being able to watch your beautiful little girl grow up is definitely a big check mark in the stay column. But honestly, I don't even know if they'll make me an offer. At this point, they just want to talk to me."

"And when is that going to happen? Have you set up a meeting?"

"Not yet. I told them I'd give the idea some thought and get back to them."

"Set up the meeting," Eloise urged. "You don't want them to think you're not interested."

"No, but I'm still waiting to hear about the grant."

Eloise sighed as she glanced down at her sleeping baby. "Apparently your aunt Charlotte would rather swim with dolphins than hear you speak your first word or watch you take your first steps."

"You know that's not true."

"Do I?"

Charlotte rolled her eyes. "I'll keep you posted—if there's anything to be posted about. In the meantime, I'm going to ask you not to say anything to Mom and Dad about this. I don't need them badgering me, too."

Eloise mimed turning a key to lock her lips.

When Charlotte parted ways with her sister and Merry back at the hotel a short while later, her first thought was to call Billy and share the news with him. Except there wasn't really any news to share. Certainly nothing definite.

And while she was excited about the potential opportunity—and the possibility of staying in Bronco and exploring a relationship with him now—he hadn't said or done anything to indicate that he saw a future for them together. Of course, he probably wasn't ready to think about a new relationship, and she'd made it clear that her stay in Bronco had an expiration date.

And while it was possible that her plans might change, she decided to wait until she knew for sure before she said anything to him.

Billy was hardly a gourmet cook, but he usually managed to put a decent meal on the table for his family. Of course, he often enlisted the kids' help with the prep and the cooking—unless he cheated and defrosted one of the meals that his mom had sent over.

Tonight, he wanted to do better than put a decent meal on the table. So he'd taken a roast out of the freezer the day before to let it thaw before applying his favorite dry rub and setting it in the slow cooker. Thankfully, when Jane left, she'd left the appliance behind. Not that he'd known what to do with it at the time, but he'd eventually figured it out and discovered the benefits of tossing a bunch of ingredients into the pot at lunchtime and finding a cooked meal in the same pot when he pulled off his boots and work gloves at the end of the day.

He had the table set and had even put wineglasses out—which was when he realized he didn't have any wine. He'd intended to pick up a bottle when he was in town, but he'd completely forgotten. *Dammit.*

He glanced at his watch.

It was already four thirty, which meant that he definitely didn't have time to go into town now. He could swing by his parents' place and borrow a bottle from their cellar, but that would undoubtedly lead to an inquiry that he wasn't in the mood for right now.

Instead, he texted his sister Robin.

I need a favor.

Twenty minutes later, she was at his door with a bottle of pinot noir—which she clutched against her chest when he reached for it.

"I have questions," she told him.

"Can I answer them tomorrow?"

"You've got company coming. Obviously."

"Obviously," he agreed.

"Charlotte?"

His parents—or at least his mom—didn't approve of him hanging out with his long-ago fiancée, but Robin had always liked Charlotte and he had no reason—aside from the whole leaving him at the altar thing—to believe that his sister's feelings had changed.

"Yes, Charlotte," he confirmed.

She handed him the bottle.

"Thanks."

"I will have more questions tomorrow," she promised.

"Just as long as you get out of here now."

"I'm going." But she paused before doing so. "Open the wine early, so it has a chance to breathe. And savor every drop, because I liberated that bottle from the top shelf."

Which they both knew was where Asa and Bonnie kept the best stuff.

As soon as his sister had gone, he opened the wine.

Then he straightened the napkins and rubbed the cutlery with a tea towel, erasing imaginary water spots.

He was nervous, he realized, aligning a knife with the plate. Charlotte's visit on Saturday night had been spontaneous, so he hadn't had a lot of time to think or worry about what might or might not happen. Tonight had been planned, and he had very high hopes for how the evening might end.

She pulled into the driveway just before five o'clock. He knew because he was watching through the curtains. But he waited until she'd knocked on the door before he made his way down the hall to open it, not wanting to appear too eager.

"Hi," she said.

"Hi," he echoed, stepping aside so that she could enter.

She offered him a bakery box. "I brought dessert."

"Cheesecake?"

She grinned. "How'd you guess?"

He helped her with her coat first, hanging it in the closet before taking the box so that she could remove her boots.

"Mmm…something smells good," Charlotte said, following him into the kitchen.

He put the bakery box in the fridge, then lowered his head to sniff her neck. "I think it's you."

She laughed softly. "I think it's whatever you've got cooking."

"No," he said, nibbling on her throat. "It's definitely you."

She took a step back, putting some space between them. Slowing things down?

Or sending him a message?

"Can I pour you a glass of wine?" he offered.

Her brows lifted. "You have wine?"

"It's a pinot noir," he said. "I don't know much about wine, but I know that's what you ordered the other night and it tasted good to me."

"A glass of wine would be nice, thanks."

He led the way to the dining room, through which she could see into the living room, now decorated for the holidays.

"You finally got a Christmas tree." She took a few steps into the room, to examine it more closely.

"The kids and I went out Sunday afternoon."

"It's beautiful," she said.

"I can't take all the credit," he said. "Or really any of the credit. I just chop it down and throw on the lights. Branson, Nicky and Jill do the rest."

"Well, they did a great job."

He offered her the glass of wine he'd poured.

"Thanks." She took a sip.

"Is it good?"

"Very good."

He lifted a hand to brush a strand of hair from her cheek.

She shivered at his touch, then took a step back again.

"You seem nervous," he noted.

"I guess I am. A little."

"I'm glad to know it's not just me."

"You're nervous, too?" She sounded dubious. "Why?"

"Because tonight seems a lot like a date, and I haven't been on a date in a very long time."

"You made it clear the other night, when you invited me for dinner, that we were just hanging out as friends."

"That was a lot easier to believe before we got naked together."

"You're right about that," she agreed.

"I don't know if this will help put you at ease or not, but I promise that we're not going to do anything you don't want to do. If you just want to talk and have dinner, that's fine."

"Really?"

"I'm not saying I won't be disappointed, but I'll survive."

She sipped her wine again. "When is dinner going to be ready?"

"The last time I checked, the timer on the slow cooker showed twenty-nine minutes left."

"Does your slow cooker automatically shift to a warm mode when the cooking time is up?"

"It does," he confirmed.

"Good." She set her glass of wine on the table, then lifted her hands to link them behind his head to draw his mouth down to hers. "Because I think we're going to need more than twenty-nine minutes."

She might have made the first move, but Billy had no trouble catching up. His tongue slid between her lips; she met it with her own. He wrapped his arms around her, drawing her closer. She gasped at the evidence of his arousal pressed against her, but she didn't pull away. Instead, she pushed her hips forward, rubbing herself against him. Heat flared between them, making him burn with a desire that threatened to consume him.

But he'd promised that nothing would happen that she didn't want to happen, and despite the fact that she'd initiated the kiss, he needed to be sure that they were on the same page.

He reluctantly eased his mouth from hers. "What are we doing here, Charlotte?"

"Hopefully, the same thing we did the other night," she said. "And you didn't have any questions then."

"Probably because I was too overwhelmed by lust to think clearly."

"You're not lusting for me now?" she challenged.

"I'm definitely lusting for you. I just want to know what this—" he gestured between them "—means."

"Do we have to put a label on it?"

"I guess not," he said dubiously.

"So why don't we just say that we're enjoying spending time together?" she suggested.

"That would certainly be true," he agreed.

"I've been looking forward to tonight ever since we said goodbye early Sunday morning," she told him. "And dreaming of you every night."

His curiosity was piqued. "Erotic dreams?"

"Very erotic dreams."

"Tell me more," he said.

Her lips curved. "Why don't I show you instead?"

Charlotte glanced at the glowing numbers on the clock on Billy's bedside table. It was after six o'clock.

"A lot more than twenty-nine minutes," she mused.

His hand slid up her torso, from her hip to her breast,

his thumb lazily teasing the peak. "Did you say something?"

"Nothing important," she said.

"Should we venture downstairs and see if that roast is completely dried out yet?" he asked.

"If you want to venture downstairs, you better stop what you're doing before you get me all stirred up again."

"I like when you're all stirred up," he said.

She grasped his wrist to pull his hand away from her breast.

Of course, he was a lot stronger than she was, and his hand didn't budge—but his lips curved.

"Is this all it takes to get you stirred up?" He continued to rub her nipple, sending sparks ricocheting through her body.

"You're playing with fire," she warned.

"Am I?" He was obviously unconcerned. "What if I did this?" he asked, and lowered his head to take her other nipple in his mouth.

A low moan sounded deep in her throat.

He responded by swirling his tongue around the turgid peak, making her squirm.

It seemed he had a talent for knowing just where and how to touch her until all conscious thought was drowned out by a wave of desire. She'd had other lovers, but no one had ever touched her the way Billy touched her. No one else had ever made her feel the way he'd made her feel—even at seventeen.

The intensity of their teenage hormones had been tempered by their love for one another, leading each of them to focus more on their partner's pleasure than their own. And while Billy had always ensured that she was satisfied, he clearly had a lot more experience at thirty-seven than he'd had at seventeen, and he gave her more pleasure now than she ever would have guessed was possible.

As his hands stroked over her, sparks danced along her veins, igniting new wants, desperate desires. He parted the slick folds of skin at the apex of her thighs, then lowered his head and put his mouth on her there. His tongue flicked over her. Slowly. Gently. Then faster. Harder.

She clutched at the sheets, desperate for something to hold onto as the world spun around her. Her heart was beating so hard and fast, she wondered that it didn't leap right out of her chest as every pass of his tongue drove her closer and closer to the edge of oblivion and finally...over.

"You were saying?" he prompted, after several minutes had passed.

"I have no idea," she admitted.

He grinned as he parted her legs further to settle between them. "Let's see what else I can make you forget."

By the time he'd finished loving her, she could barely remember her own name. It was only when her stomach growled that she remembered they hadn't yet had dinner.

"You're hungry," Billy realized.

"A little," she admitted.

"Well, I'm starving," he said. "I haven't worked out like that since..."

"Saturday night?" she suggested.

He grinned again. "Yeah."

"Well, you're definitely not out of shape," she said, sliding her hands over the ridged muscles of his stomach.

"I like your shape, too," he said. "Every dip and curve."

He touched his mouth to hers again, kissing her so deeply and thoroughly it made her head spin.

Or maybe she was dizzy with hunger.

"Food," she reminded him, when he finally eased his mouth from hers.

"Right." He rolled away from her and off the bed, reaching for his jeans.

Charlotte gathered up her scattered clothing and began to dress. "What time will the kids be home?"

"I don't expect them before ten," Billy said, shrugging into his shirt. "Jane mentioned wanting to take them to Wonderstone Ridge to see the big display of Christmas lights."

His mention of the nearby town gave her pause.

It seemed an odd coincidence—or maybe it was a sign—that he'd mentioned Wonderstone Ridge when she'd been contemplating whether or not to say anything about the phone call she'd received two days earlier.

A sign, she decided, and opened her mouth to tell him about the potential job.

Before she could do so, he said, "Don't worry about putting all your clothes back on—it will only take me longer to get them off you later."

"If we weren't going to be having dinner in the house you live in with your three minor children, I'd happily sit at the table half-naked," she told him. "But since those children could walk through the door at any time—"

"I told you, they'll be gone for hours yet," Billy reassured her.

"Still," she said, as she finished buttoning her shirt. "I'd rather be safe than sorry."

"I'd rather see you at the table half-naked."

"Another time perhaps."

"I'll look forward to it," he promised, taking her hand and leading her back down the stairs.

Chapter Thirteen

Charlotte topped off their wineglasses while Billy sliced the beef, serving it with sides of roasted potatoes and carrots topped with au jus. She was impressed not only by the presentation of the food but the effort he'd expended in preparing it for her. And that was before she sampled the meal.

"This is really good," she said, dabbing another piece of roast in the au jus.

"It's the rub," he said.

"Yeah, that was pretty spectacular, but I'm not sure what it has to do with dinner."

He shook his head, but he was smiling. "I was referring to the dry spice mix I use on the meat. The roast," he was quick to clarify, before she could follow up with another double entendre.

"Did you do much cooking when you were married?" she asked.

"Not much," he admitted. "Usually only once a week— on Saturday nights—to give Jane a break. I'd try to get the kids to help out, too. Jill was more willing than the boys, but I made them do their share, too. Though they're better at cleaning up than cooking.

"I took for granted how much Jane did around the house, so I'm determined to ensure that they don't do the same. That they're capable of taking care of themselves—not just cooking their own meals but doing laundry and scrubbing toilets."

"Their future partners will thank you," Charlotte assured him.

"Honestly, I think Jill tries to do a little too much. It's as if she's taken on the role of woman of the house since her mom left—and she's only thirteen."

She sipped her wine. "And how do they get along with their mom's new boyfriend?"

"Reluctantly," he said. "Or at least that's the impression I get. It could be they think he's great but they don't want me to know for fear of seeming disloyal."

"A colleague of mine split from his wife a couple years back—her choice. She didn't see any point in being married when they hardly ever saw one another because he was moving from research station to research station. Since then, he's missed their seven-year-old daughter like crazy. So he finally stopped traveling as much, and now they're talking about reconciling."

He laid his fork on the table and sat back. "I'm sure you had a reason for sharing that story about people

I don't know, but I can't figure out what it is," he admitted.

"I guess I was just wondering if you'd given any thought to the possibility of getting back together with your ex-wife."

"No."

"That was a pretty emphatic response," she noted.

"Aside from the fact that she's now in a relationship with someone else, why would I want to get back together with her?"

"For the kids?"

"Who will start leaving home over the next few years."

She felt relieved by his response—and then guilty for being glad that his marriage was definitively over. Which didn't make any sense, because he'd already been divorced before she returned to Bronco. And because whatever his future looked like, she didn't know if there was a place for her in it.

But she was starting to hope that there could be.

"The truth is, I'm not sure we ever should have gotten married," he continued. "I don't regret the years I spent with her, because she gave me Branson, Nicky and Jill, and there aren't any words that can express how much my kids mean to me. But Jane wasn't wrong when she said I never loved her as much as she loved me."

"You obviously loved her enough to want to marry her."

"I wanted a wife and a family, and she seemed to want the same things I did—until she didn't."

"I'm sorry things didn't work out," she said sincerely.

He shrugged. "I'm getting used to handling the day-to-day stuff on my own. The holidays are harder. And I'm definitely not looking forward to being on my own on Christmas Day.

"But I won't be alone the whole day," he said. "My mom will cook a big meal around lunchtime, and then a friend of mine is getting married later in the afternoon, so that will get me out of the house for a while."

"You have a friend who's getting married on Christmas Day?"

Billy nodded.

"Is he by any chance marrying Sadie Chamberlin?"

"How could you know that?"

"It was a guess," she confided. "But I knew that Sadie was getting married on the twenty-fifth—because she invited me—and I didn't think it was likely that there would be more than one wedding in town on that day."

"Are you going to the wedding?"

"That's my plan," she confirmed.

"Then I guess I'll see you there."

Charlotte was a little disappointed that he didn't suggest they go together, though she understood that he might be reluctant to make a public statement about their relationship so soon.

Billy held the bottle of wine. "Can I pour you another glass?"

"I don't think I should," she said regretfully. "I have to drive home."

"I wish you didn't have to go."

"Me, too," she said, pushing away from the table.

"But you don't have to go just yet," he said, rising to his feet, too.

"Not right this minute," she agreed. "I've probably got time for a slice of that cheesecake."

"Cheesecake, huh?" He pulled her into his arms and kissed her again.

They were still kissing when Billy heard the click of the front door unlocking.

He reluctantly lifted his mouth from Charlotte's to glance at his watch.

8:38.

What the—

"Dad! We're home!"

Charlotte pulled out of his arms and retreated to her seat at the table, as if she'd just finished eating.

"In the dining room," he called back.

"Whose car is—" Jill abruptly cut off her own question when she saw Charlotte seated at the table. Her smile faded. "Oh. Miss Taylor."

"Hello, Jill." She nodded to the boys who followed in their sister's footsteps, albeit at a more leisurely pace. "Branson. Nicky."

The boys mumbled "hello" in response.

Jill continued to frown, obviously unhappy to find that her dad wasn't alone.

Billy glanced at Charlotte, relieved that she'd put all her clothes back on before leaving his bedroom. But her hair was slightly tousled from their lovemaking and her lips swollen from his kisses. Not that he expected his thirteen-year-old daughter to pick up on any of those clues, but he suspected that her older brothers might.

Not to mention that if any of them peeked into his bedroom, they'd likely discover the covers were rumpled—if they were even still on the bed. And while he didn't want to advertise the nature of his relationship with Charlotte, he wasn't going to hide her away from his kids, either.

"You're home early," Billy remarked.

"I'm playing D&D online with my friends at nine o'clock," Nicky said.

Which he definitely hadn't mentioned to his father before now. In fact—

"I thought Thursday was D&D night."

"Usually," Nicky agreed. "But Dallas has some family thing tomorrow, so we switched it to tonight."

"You had a family thing tonight," Billy pointed out.

"Dinner with Mom and Henri is hardly a family thing," Branson scoffed.

"Is it a problem that we're home early?" Jill asked, her tone cool. "Are we interrupting something?"

"No," he was quick to assure them.

Though if they'd returned an hour or so earlier, they definitely would have been.

"Are you hungry?" Charlotte asked them. "Your dad made a delicious pot roast."

"We ate," Jill said shortly. "With our mom."

"Did she cook or did you go out?" Billy asked.

"She's trying her hand at French cooking," Branson said with an eye roll.

"We had coco ven," Jill said.

It took Billy a moment to translate that to *coq au vin*.

"Did you enjoy it?" Charlotte asked politely.

Nicky shrugged. "It was all right."

"I thought it was *delicious*," Jill said, deliberately

choosing the same word Charlotte had used to describe his roast.

"Did you go to Wonderstone Ridge to see the Christmas lights?" Billy asked.

"Mom wanted to," Branson said. "But Nicky didn't want to be late for D&D."

"Which I need to set up for," Nicky said, and made his escape.

Charlotte glanced at her watch. "I had no idea it was so late already."

"I guess time flies when you're having fun," Branson remarked.

She pushed her chair away from the table and picked up her plate.

"I'll take that for you," Jill said, pretending to be helpful in an obvious effort to nudge Charlotte along. "You probably need to be getting home."

"I'd like to help your dad with the cleanup, to show my appreciation for the meal."

"No need," Jill said. "I'll give him a hand."

She looked at Billy.

"You don't need to rush off," he told her.

"I think maybe I do."

Obviously this wasn't how either of them wanted the evening to end, but apparently the choice had been taken out of their hands.

"Thanks, Jill," he said to his daughter. "Why don't you get started while I walk Charlotte out to her car?"

"I don't think she's going to get lost between here and there."

"I'll be right back," he promised, again choosing to ignore her remark—and her acidic tone.

Charlotte was already at the door, putting on her boots. He helped her with her coat, then grabbed his own.

"I'm sorry about that," he said, as they stepped onto the porch, closing the door behind them.

"There's no need to apologize," she told him, starting toward her vehicle. "But it's apparent they don't like seeing you with a woman who isn't their mom."

"Because they've never seen me with a woman who isn't their mom," he confided.

"Which means you're going to get the third degree when you go back inside," she warned.

"Another reason to stay out here with you as long as possible," he said, reaching for her.

Charlotte stepped back, opening the door of her SUV and putting it between them.

"I don't get a kiss goodbye?"

"I'm probably sorrier than you are," she told him. "But I'd bet that Branson and Jill are peeking through the curtains and I don't want to make the situation any more awkward for you."

"So tell me when I can see you again," he suggested.

"I think we're both going to be busy over the next several days," she said regretfully.

"Give me a call if you find yourself with any free time. I'll pick you up and take you parking. Like the old days."

"I just might have to take you up on that offer."

He smiled. "I sincerely hope you do." Then, despite

her earlier protest, he leaned over the open door to brush a quick kiss on her lips. "Drive safe."

If his kids had been peeking through the curtains, they'd hurried back to the kitchen by the time he returned to the house.

"Thanks for your help," he said to Jill, who was washing up dishes.

She lifted her hands out of the soapy water and dried them on a towel before turning to face him. "Are you *dating* her?" she asked, obviously unhappy to consider the possibility.

"No, we're not dating," he said.

Because he didn't think a couple of shared meals and a couple of hook-ups counted as dating. But really, what did he know? He hadn't dated anyone since he'd dated Jane, more than eighteen years earlier.

"Charlotte's a friend from way back," he reminded her.

"You made dinner for her. With wine." Her tone was accusatory.

"So?"

"So it looks a lot like a date," Branson noted.

"I don't understand why you're giving me a hard time about spending time with a friend," he said, irritated by their judgment. "Especially you, Jill. I thought you liked Miss Taylor."

"I did—when she was *Miss Taylor*. Now all of a sudden she's *Charlotte* and you're having romantic dinners with her while we're out of the house."

"It was one dinner," he said. "Next time, I'll invite her to come over when you're here."

"No, thank you." She stomped out of the room.

He scrubbed his hands over his face.

Branson remained where he was, studying him.

"What?" Billy asked.

His elder son shrugged. "I was just thinking that if you'd made half as much effort for Mom, she might not have left."

Ouch.

"You might be right," Billy admitted, dipping his hands into the sink to pick up where Jill had left off. "Sometimes, when a couple is married a long time, they start to take one another for granted. And I did that with your mom, even if I didn't realize it at the time."

"Did she ever try to talk to you about it?" Branson asked.

"No. I don't think so." He sighed again. "Maybe."

Branson frowned as he opened the pantry door and pulled out a jar of peanut butter. "You don't know?"

"We talked about a lot of things that I probably didn't pay enough attention to because I was preoccupied with ranch business. I know she was at a loss about what to do with herself as you guys got older and grew more independent."

He drained the sink and folded the cloth, remembering that he'd been all for Jane taking a French class—whatever made her happy. He just didn't expect it would be the French teacher that made her happy.

"I guess we didn't communicate well," he added for his son's sake.

Branson frowned at that as he started spreading peanut butter on a slice of bread.

"Packing your lunch?" Billy guessed.

"Making a snack," his son clarified.

"You didn't like the coq au vin?"

"Apparently French food is all about fancy names and tiny portions."

Billy frowned. "I'm sure you could have asked for a second helping."

"I didn't want to give Mom the impression that it was good."

"It wasn't?"

"Not my kind of food," Branson said.

"In that case, I'll bet your brother's hungry, too."

"Nicky can make his own sandwich," Branson said, already biting into his.

Billy reached into the cupboard over the sink for a glass, filled it with milk and handed it to his son.

"Thanks." Branson took the sandwich and drink to the table.

"Any plans for the next couple of days?" Billy asked, curious to know what his eldest planned to do with his time now that school was finished until the New Year.

"I figured I'd help out wherever you need it around the ranch."

"I appreciate it," Billy said, starting to make another sandwich. "If you don't mind, I'd also like you to take your brother and sister into town—or the Valley—to do some Christmas shopping."

"You want us to get something for Mom?" Branson guessed.

He nodded. "You can't show up empty-handed on the twenty-fifth."

"Do we really have to spend Christmas Day with her and Henri?" His son's tone was glum.

"I'm not any happier about it than you are," Billy assured him. "But I got Thanksgiving this year, so she gets Christmas. Next year, it'll be the opposite."

"So when are we going to celebrate Christmas here?" Branson asked.

"Christmas Eve."

"Are you going to cook a turkey?"

"I'm going to try."

"Maybe you could invite Grandma and Grandpa to join us," his son suggested.

"You think if I do, Grandma will offer to cook the turkey," Billy guessed.

Branson shrugged. "It's worth a shot."

"Except that she's already cooking a big meal on Christmas Day. I'm not going to ask her to do it two days in a row."

"I guess that makes sense," his son agreed.

"Besides, I know I can count on you and your brother and sister to give me a hand. And you've gotten really good at peeling potatoes."

"Not that good," Branson was quick to protest.

"Then it will be an opportunity to practice."

His son sighed. "You had me cornered there, didn't you?"

"A little bit," he agreed with a grin.

He left Branson to finish his snack while he carried the other sandwich and a second glass of milk upstairs to Nicky. He knocked on the door, then balanced the plate on top of the glass to twist the knob and enter when given the signal to do so.

"Don't spill the milk on your keyboard," he cautioned, setting the plate and glass on the desk.

Nicky tapped a button to silence his microphone long enough to say a quick "Thanks, Dad" before he returned his attention to his friends.

Billy made his way across the hall to knock on Jill's door.

"What?"

Not exactly an invitation but better than the "go away" he'd half expected as her response.

He turned the knob and stepped inside her room, pausing when he spotted the blank space on her wall. The previous weekend, she'd bought a dolphin poster when she was shopping with Alyssa. She'd even taken down her BTS poster to put the dolphins in their place. Now the dolphin poster was crumpled up in the garbage.

"Do you want to talk?" he asked her.

"Is there something to talk about?"

"I'd like to know why you're so bothered by the fact that I invited Charlotte over for dinner."

Her eyes filled with tears, but she glanced away quickly, as if she didn't want him to see them. "Because everything is changing."

He perched on the edge of her bed.

She drew her knees up to her chest—literally pulling away from him.

"Change isn't always a bad thing," he told her.

"No?" she challenged. "Tell me how you felt when your mom and dad got divorced."

"Obviously I can't," he acknowledged.

"Because they got married and stayed married and you didn't have to spend one weekend with your dad and the next with your mom."

"I know it's not an ideal situation, but it was the best way to ensure that your mom and I both get to spend time with you and your brothers."

"She could have spent a lot more time with us if she'd stayed here," Jill pointed out.

"She wasn't happy here," he said gently.

"So maybe you should have tried harder to make her happy."

Apparently that was the theme of tonight's conversations with his kids—his failings as a husband.

"Maybe I should have," he agreed. "And maybe I would have if I'd realized she was unhappy."

"Instead, she screwed around on you."

His jaw tightened. "I get that you're upset about the divorce, but I'm not going to tolerate you speaking that way about your mother."

"Why not? It's the truth, isn't it?"

He didn't know if she'd overheard gossip at school or simply put two and two together based on the fact that Jane had moved out of their house and in with Henri.

"I understand that your life has been turned upside down through no fault of your own and it doesn't seem fair. And you're right," Billy said. "It's not fair. But we can't change the situation, so we have to make the best of it."

"And now you're making the best of it with Charlotte?"

"I'm not going to apologize for spending time with Charlotte," he told her. "Because, believe it or not, the divorce has been hard on me, too."

"Because you miss Mom?" she asked hopefully.

"Because I miss you and your brothers," he said. "And when you're not here, the house is really quiet. So I invited Charlotte to come over so I had someone to talk to."

"I guess I can understand that," she finally said. "But why couldn't you invite Uncle Theo or Uncle Jace?"

"Because I see Uncle Theo and Uncle Jace every day on the ranch," he reminded her. "And because Charlotte's a lot prettier than they are."

She scowled at that. "You really think she's pretty?"

"I do," he confirmed.

"Prettier than Mom?"

"It's not a contest, Jill."

"But if it was a contest—"

"Nope," he interjected. "We're not playing that game."

She sighed. "I just wish you still loved Mom."

"I will always love your mom for giving me you and Nicky and Branson."

She considered that for a minute before saying, "But mostly me, right? Because Nicky and Branson are gross."

He chuckled softly and shifted on the bed, holding out his arms. "Come here."

After a brief hesitation, she crawled into his arms.

"I love you, Jilly Bean." he told her. Because the divorce had meant a lot of changes for all of them, but he wanted his daughter to know that his feelings for her would never diminish.

"I love you, too, Daddy."

After he'd savored her hug for a moment, he asked, "Are you hungry?"

"I could go for some popcorn," she decided.

"And a movie?" he guessed.

She tipped her head back to look at him. "How about *Elf*?"

"Didn't we watch that one last year?"

"We watch it every year," she agreed. "That's what makes it a tradition."

"Well, Nicky's wrapped up in his game and Branson's on the phone with Courtney, so it might just be you and me tonight."

"I'm okay with that," Jill said.

And so was he.

Chapter Fourteen

"Are you busy tonight?"

Charlotte looked up to see her brother Seth standing in the doorway of the dining room where she was wrapping presents late Thursday afternoon. "Do I not look busy?" she asked him.

"That doesn't look like anything that can't wait," he said.

"What do you need?"

"Someone with bony elbows to nudge me if I start to fall asleep watching *It Came Upon a Midnight Clear*."

"Isn't that the name of the play that the Bronco Theater Company is putting on this year?"

He nodded. "Opening night is tonight."

"And you bought tickets?"

"Yeah." The admission was made reluctantly.

"Why?"

"Because I've kind of been seeing this woman who's in it, and it seemed to be a big deal to her for me to be there."

"Who is this woman and why am I only hearing about her now?" Charlotte asked her brother.

"Her name is Felicia and you're only hearing about her now because I've hardly seen you since you got home," he said in response to her questions.

A fair point, she acknowledged.

"How long have you been seeing her?"

"A couple of months. It's not serious."

"Serious enough to have you going to the theater," she couldn't resist teasing.

"Are you in or not?"

She glanced at her watch. "What time is curtain?"

"Seven thirty."

"Okay," she said. Because she knew that if she stayed home, she'd keep looking at her phone, hoping to hear from Billy.

Though it had been less than twenty-four hours since she last saw him, it somehow felt longer—and as if there was a distance between them that was growing.

She was probably overreacting to the less-than-warm welcome she'd received from his kids when they'd come home and found her with their dad, but she knew that if Branson, Nicky and Jill were opposed to him being involved with her, it would be a serious obstacle to their relationship.

And since she really didn't want to sit home and obsess about what might or might not happen, an eve-

ning at the Bronco Theater sounded like a wonderful
distraction.

"But you have to buy me dinner first," she added.

"Why can't we have dinner here?" Seth asked her.

"Because it's Lina's night off and Mom's making
Salisbury steak."

That was apparently enough to convince him, because he asked, "What are you in the mood for?"

"Maybe a burger that isn't swimming in gravy?"
she suggested.

"Well, then, you better go get ready," he said. "I'll
call DJ's Deluxe and see if I can snag us a table."

It didn't take her long to get ready. She simply
swapped her jeans and sweater for a pair of wool pants
and a silky blouse, added some chunky jewelry borrowed from her mother, brushed her hair, added a swipe
of mascara and a dab of lip gloss.

"You look pretty good, sis," Seth said, when she met
him downstairs.

"So do you," she remarked, reaching up to straighten
his tie. "Not serious, huh?"

"Not serious," he confirmed.

"And yet you're wearing a tie."

"Not for the theater," he said. "For the restaurant."

"Are you telling me this burger place has a dress
code?"

"DJ's Deluxe has a lot more than burgers," he told
her. "I'm surprised you haven't been there before, but I
guess it's only been open a few years and you don't come
home very often."

"Swimming with the dolphins is a tough job, but somebody's gotta do it."

"I know you do a lot more than swim with dolphins," Seth said.

"Not according to Dad," she remarked wryly.

"He'd never say it to you, but he's proud of you," her brother told her.

"He's definitely never said that to me."

"But he says it to anyone who sits down with him at The Association."

"Really?"

Seth nodded. "Of course, he also tells them that you would have been better off studying dinosaurs, because at least you might find some of their bones in Montana."

"Yeah, that sounds more like dear old Dad," she agreed.

He looped an arm across her shoulders. "C'mon. We've got a six o'clock reservation."

"So tell me about this play," Charlotte said to her brother, as she followed him into the theater.

"I don't know a lot about it, except that the script was written by our cousin Dean's wife, Susanna, and it's billed as a family-friendly holiday romance," Seth told her.

"And what part does Felicia play?"

"She's the heroine's archenemy—and the sister of the hero."

"Oooh, archenemy, huh?"

He shrugged. "Apparently."

"Sounds like a juicy part."

"I guess we'll see."

She scanned the program and learned that the name of the character Felicia played was "Star."

From their seats in the third row, she could see the actors clearly—and it wasn't hard for her to see why her brother was attracted to Felicia. The actor was very pretty. And very young.

"She looks about twenty," she hissed to Seth, the first time "Star" appeared onstage.

"Twenty-eight," he whispered back.

"Which is younger than your youngest sister," she pointed out to him.

"So?"

"So you're forty."

"And you're thirty-seven—and still sneaking out of your bedroom window like you did when you were a teenager."

She frowned. "Why would you think I snuck out?"

He gave her a look. "I don't think, I know. Ryan saw you on Saturday night."

"Our little brother always was a tattletale," she muttered, not entirely under her breath. "Okay, if you promise not to tell anyone else that I snuck out, I'll stop nagging you about the fact that you're dating a woman younger than your youngest sister."

"Deal," he agreed.

And they settled in to focus on the play.

The story was somewhat predictable but still enjoyable, and Charlotte couldn't help but be impressed by the talent of the local cast.

Her brother was a little less impressed—or maybe he

was just tired because, as a rancher, he was up with the sun every day. Whatever the reason, she had to elbow him three times. Twice because his eyes were starting to drift closed and the third time just because.

After the curtain calls, Charlotte waited in the lobby while Seth went backstage to congratulate Felicia on her performance. He returned a few minutes later and said, "I need you to get a ride home."

"Are you kidding?"

"Come on, sis," he cajoled. "This place is packed. There must be someone you know who can drop you off at Mom and Dad's."

"I should take your truck and leave you stranded," she muttered.

"You could—except that I've got the keys." He dangled them out of her reach.

She glared at him. "Last time I do you a favor."

"Don't think I don't know that last elbow was just for fun. And after I bought you dinner, too."

"You don't go anywhere until you know I've got a ride home."

"Don't take too long," he said. "Felicia is eager to celebrate."

"With the rest of the cast?" she asked with feigned innocence.

"Look—there's Asa and Bonnie Abernathy."

He started to lift his hand, as if to get their attention.

She grabbed his arm and yanked it down.

"Forget it," she said. "I'll call a cab."

"Why do you need a cab?" a voice asked from behind her.

Charlotte turned and found herself facing another pair of Abernathys—Robin and Stacy—Billy's sisters.

"They're everywhere," Seth murmured under his breath.

She glared at him over her shoulder before turning back to respond to Robin's question. "To take me back to my parents' place."

"We can drop you off," the other woman immediately offered.

"It's not exactly on our way," Stacy grumbled.

"It's not too far out of our way, either," her sister argued.

"Maybe a cab would be a better idea," Charlotte said, not wanting to be the cause of any more friction within the Abernathy family.

"Don't be silly." Robin linked her arm through Charlotte's. "The drive will give you a chance to tell me how much you enjoyed the Aubert pinot noir."

"Mom sent over a chicken pot pie," Stacy said, when Billy opened the door and found his sister standing on his porch.

"I already have three in my freezer."

"Now you'll have four." Instead of waiting for him to take the foil-covered glass dish from her, she sidled past him and into the foyer.

"Please, come in," he said dryly.

"Thanks." She wiped her boots on the mat then made her way to the mudroom to set the pie in the chest freezer. "I've got time for a cup of coffee."

"You know where it is," he told her.

She shrugged out of her coat and hung it on a hook by the door before heading to the kitchen.

"I see you finally found your Christmas spirit," she said, glancing into the living room.

"Or at least the decorations," he noted.

She reached into the cupboard for a mug, filled it with coffee from the carafe on the warmer. "Why's it so quiet? Where are the kids?"

"Apparently Christmas break is all about sleeping in."

"Ah, to be a teenager again," she said wistfully.

He refilled his own mug of coffee, waiting for his sister to get around to the point of her visit. Because Stacy always had a point—and he knew that the pie was an excuse rather than a reason.

"There was a car I didn't recognize in your driveway the other night," she finally said.

He sipped his coffee. "Is that a statement or a question?"

"Was Charlotte here?" she asked, cutting to the chase.

"Yes."

Stacy scowled—and looked a lot like her niece in doing so. "Are you two an item again?"

"We're friends."

"Friends who have sex?"

He was grateful that the kids were still sleeping and not able to overhear this conversation. "My relationship with Charlotte isn't any of your business."

"So it is a relationship."

"Not any of your business," he said again.

"She ditched you at the altar."

"Twenty years ago."

She was silent for a minute before confiding, "Robin and I ran into her last night. At the theater."

He sipped his coffee again.

"We gave her a ride home, after her date left her stranded."

"Her date?" he echoed, and immediately cursed himself for taking the bait she'd dangled.

"Her brother," Stacy acknowledged.

Billy was more relieved than he wanted to admit.

"Robin thinks you've still got a thing for her. I told her that she's wrong."

"I'm glad you and Robin entertain yourselves discussing my personal life."

"We're worried about you."

"No need," he assured her.

She sighed. "Are you going to invite her to Christmas dinner?"

"No."

"Well, that's good then," Stacy said.

"There's no point in sending Mom into a tizzy when Charlotte's only going to be in town another couple of weeks."

His sister frowned. "Is that true?"

"That's what she told me."

"When did she tell you that?"

"Last week. Why?"

"Because I heard that her plans might have changed."

"Did her grant come through?" He hoped, for Charlotte's sake, that it had, because he knew how much her work meant to her. But he'd selfishly hoped for more time with her. In fact, he'd been planning to ask her to spend New Year's Eve with him. Branson, Nicky and Jill would be there, too, but he wanted to ring in the New Year surrounded by all the people he lov—

"I don't know anything about a grant," Stacy said, interrupting his thoughts. "But I was at the new Hey, Baby store looking for a gift for Frankie when I ran into one of my colleagues—Dante Sanchez. He was there with his girlfriend—Charlotte's youngest sister—and I overheard Eloise mention to him that Charlotte has been offered a job at the marine discovery center being built in Wonderstone Ridge."

"When was this?"

"Yesterday." Stacy eyed him closely. "She didn't say anything to you about it?"

"No," he admitted.

His sister shrugged. "So maybe Eloise is wrong."

Or maybe Charlotte hasn't said anything to Billy about the job because she had no interest in working in Wonderstone Ridge or staying in Bronco.

And why did it matter?

He'd been under no illusions that she was going to stay.

She'd told him that she was leaving after the holidays, so he hadn't let himself think beyond that.

Of course, it was possible that his sister had misinterpreted what Eloise said.

Or maybe Eloise had misinterpreted what Charlotte told her.

But the fact that there was something to misinterpret, and that Charlotte hadn't said a word to him—not even when he'd told her that the kids were supposed to be going to Wonderstone Ridge to see the lights—spoke volumes.

Thinking back on that conversation, he remembered that she'd paused at his mention of the nearby town, as if there was something she wanted to say. But in the end, she'd remained silent.

Because she had no intention—obviously no desire—to stay in Bronco.

No interest in staying with him.

It shouldn't bother him, because she'd already made it clear that she would be leaving in January. But it did, because somehow, in the space of only a few days, he'd fallen head over heels for her again—and she was going to leave him again.

And if there was a viable job option on the table, it wasn't because she had to leave, but because she didn't want to stay.

Talk about déjà vu.

At least this time he wouldn't be standing in a church, dressed like a groom waiting for his bride.

Still, he knew that a second abandonment wouldn't hurt any less than the first, and there was only way to be sure she didn't leave him again.

He had to be the one to end things.

Chapter Fifteen

Charlotte had a wonderful time with her mom on Friday. They went into town to deliver their "Toys for Tots" to the community volunteers, then they got cookies and hot cocoa from Kendra's Cupcakes and enjoyed their snack while listening to the children's choir sing Christmas carols by the enormous tree in the park, and after that they stopped by the Heights Hotel for a quick visit with Eloise and Merry.

On their way back to the Triple T, Charlotte's happy day was made even happier when she got a text message from Billy, asking if she had time to meet him.

So after delivering her mom to the ranch, she drove back into town, smiling as she remembered his offer to take her parking—like the old days. They'd spent a lot of nights fogging up the windows of his truck back then, and while she didn't think he really wanted to make out like a couple of teenagers, she wouldn't object to snuggling close to stay warm on such a cold day.

She pulled into the parking lot behind the high school—totally deserted now that the students and teachers were on their holiday break—and immediately recognized his truck, parked at the far end near the football field. She pulled up beside him and slid out of the driver's seat of her vehicle and into the passenger seat of his.

"This is a nice surprise," she said, smiling at him.

Billy didn't smile back.

"I'm glad you could make it," he said. "I wasn't sure if you'd have plans—considering it's only three days before Christmas."

"If I'd had plans, I would gladly have broken them to spend a few hours with you."

"This isn't going to take that long."

An uneasy feeling stirred in the pit of her belly. "What's not going to take that long?"

"Our talk."

"You invited me to meet you here…to talk?"

He nodded.

"About what?"

"I've been doing a lot of thinking over the past couple of days, and I've decided that we should take a step back."

The unease began to spread through her body, chilling her bones far more than the outside temperature had done. "I don't understand."

"It's almost Christmas," he pointed out.

"I'm aware of that," she assured him.

"And it's going to be tough on Branson, Nicky and Jill this year—the first year that the whole family won't be together."

She could absolutely empathize with the fact that it was a tough situation, if not a particularly unique one. But— "What does that have to do with us?"

He stared straight ahead out the windshield. "Is there an us? Or were we just putting in time until you go back to the Bahamas?"

"I thought we were enjoying spending time together," she said cautiously.

"Sure, we had fun," he said. "But I have to think about my kids. I can't upend their lives any more than I've already done for the sake of a short-term fling."

"A fling," she echoed, surprised how much it hurt to hear him so easily dismiss what they'd shared.

"You're the one who kept reminding me that you're leaving in the New Year," he pointed out to her.

Because she'd wanted them both to know that there was a time limit on anything that happened between them.

But that was before.

Before they'd made love.

And before she'd gotten the call from Sean McCaffrey of the Seaway Group in Wonderstone Ridge.

And though she'd had reasons—good and valid reasons, she thought—for keeping that information to herself, maybe it was time to tell him about that call.

"Actually, that was something—"

"And I realized there's no point in continuing down this path when we both know where it's going to end," he said, forging ahead with no regard to what she was saying—or attempting to say.

She tried to draw in a breath, but her chest suddenly felt tight. She rubbed a hand over her ribs.

No, it wasn't her chest that hurt, she realized, but her heart.

"Are you…breaking up with me?"

"I'm merely moving things along to their inevitable conclusion."

She swallowed. "How do you know it's inevitable?"

"Because my life is here and yours isn't," he said matter-of-factly.

"What if things could be different?" she asked him.

He shook his head. "I'm not going to play that game. The stakes are too high—especially for my family."

"The stakes are high for me, too," she felt compelled to point out.

"But we both knew you were going to be gone in January, regardless of what happened between us."

"When I came back to Bronco, I didn't anticipate that anything would happen between us," she confided. "But this past week—it's changed everything for me."

"Well, it hasn't changed anything for me."

"But something did," she realized. "Something happened between Wednesday night and today to change your feelings about me."

"I have to get back to the ranch," he said. "The kids are going to be wondering where I am."

And clearly, that was that.

At least as far as he was concerned.

And though this wasn't at all how she wanted things

to end, it was clear that they were done—and she wasn't going to beg him to change his mind.

Instead, she reached for the handle and opened the door, pausing when her feet were on the ground only long enough to say, "Merry Christmas, Billy." Then she closed the door between them and turned away.

Her hands were trembling—everything inside her was trembling—as she got into her SUV and pulled out her phone to text her sister.

Are you still at the hotel?

She had to wait a minute for her sister's reply.

No. We're out running errands.

Would you mind if I went to your suite to hang out for a bit?

Of course not. What's going on? Do you want me to come back?

No. I just need to be alone for a little while.

You'll fill me in later.

She didn't think the lack of a question mark was a typo. Eloise obviously expected Charlotte to share all the details. And truthfully, she needed to talk to someone and was glad her sister was willing to be her confidante.

Okay. Later.

Love you, sis.

Her eyes filled with tears.

Love you, too.

She tucked her phone into her purse again and turned toward the hotel. When she got to her sister's suite, she made a cup of tea in the Keurig, then pulled her phone out again to check her email, hoping for an update on the grant.

Nothing.

No missed phone calls, no text messages.

She'd been certain they would get the funding they needed to continue their project. They were doing good work—necessary work. And she was always passionate about the plight of the oceans and the survival of dolphin species in particular, but right now, everything inside her was numb.

Which was better than hurting, she supposed.

She just wished she understood what had happened—how things with Billy had gone so wrong so quickly.

Everything had been good when she'd left his house less than forty-eight hours earlier. Well, aside from his kids having made it clear they weren't thrilled to find their dad hanging out with her. But she'd been confident their feelings would change once they got to know her. Except that Billy apparently wasn't willing to give them that chance.

She understood that he might feel torn between what he wanted and what his kids wanted. She also understood that his kids were his priority—and she would never expect anything different.

But she didn't believe his kids were the sole reason for his sudden decision to "take a step back" or, conversely, "move things along to their inevitable conclusion." And it hurt more than she could have imagined to discover that everything they'd shared this past week had meant nothing to him.

She was mostly cried out by the time Eloise and Merry got back to the hotel nearly an hour later.

"Where's Dante?" Charlotte asked, after her sister had settled the sleeping baby in her bassinet.

"He dropped us off and went back out to get the cat food we forgot."

"You have a cat?" She certainly hadn't seen any evidence of a pet on her previous visits.

"No, but Dante does," Eloise said. "Sort of."

"How do you 'sort of' have a cat?" Charlotte wondered.

"It's a stray orange tabby that he found near his apartment and started putting out food for. Which, of course, led to it hanging around more. So when he moved in here with me, he took it over to his parents' place because he didn't trust his brother to remember to feed it."

"You've got a good man there," she said to her sister.

"The best," Eloise agreed. "Though I had to kiss a few frogs before I found my prince."

"I never wanted a prince—and maybe that's my problem. I only ever wanted Billy. Even when I was more than two thousand miles away, in the middle of the Caribbean Sea, I wanted a Montana rancher."

"So what happened?"

"He decided that whatever was between us wasn't worth the effort—especially since I'm not going to stick around for the long term."

"Have you decided against applying for the job at Wonderstone Ridge then?" Eloise asked, not even attempting to hide her disappointment.

"No. In fact, I was leaning toward going for an interview and learning more about the job. Now... I don't know."

"Did you tell Billy about the job?"

"No," she said again. "I mean, I tried to, when he started talking about how we had no future together, but he didn't seem to want to hear anything I had to say."

"I'm so sorry, Charlotte."

"Me, too."

"But I hope you won't let what happened with Billy dissuade you from interviewing at the marine discovery center."

"I won't and it hasn't," she assured her sister. "I learned long ago not to let anyone else's expectations influence my life decisions. Plus, you played the baby card."

"The baby card?" Eloise echoed quizzically.

She nodded. "I want to be here to see Merry take

her first steps and hear her speak her first words. And, just so you can't say I didn't warn you, I'm going to coach her intently in the hope that those words will be 'Aunt Charlotte.'"

Eloise laughed. "You have no idea how happy I am to hear that you want to stay. And Mom and Dad are going to be over the moon."

"I still haven't said anything to them about this, because nothing is definite yet. But I'm going to give Sean McCaffrey a call right now to let him know that I'm interested in interviewing for the job."

She was reaching for her phone when it pinged to indicate receipt of a text message.

Fool that she was, her heart skipped a beat anticipating—*hoping*—it might be from Billy. That he was reaching out to tell her he'd made a horrible mistake. That as soon as he got home, he'd realized he loved her and didn't want to lose her again.

Of course, the message wasn't from Billy but from her boss.

She swiped to open the message and felt her heart lift a little.

"We got it," she said to Eloise.

"Got what?" her sister asked.

"The grant. The Dolphin Harbour Project is now funded for another five years."

"What does that mean for you?" Eloise asked cautiously.

"It means they won't have any trouble filling my position," she said, happy to know it was true.

Dante returned a short while later and Eloise jumped

up to get ready for dinner at his parents' place. Charlotte had taken that as her cue to head back to the Triple T, but her sister refused to hear it, insisting that she stay at the hotel and relax.

"Or you could come with us," Dante said. "My parents would be happy to set another place at the table."

"They would," Eloise confirmed. "Aaron and Denise are incredibly warm and welcoming people."

"Uncle Stanley is supposed to be there tonight, too."

"And he rarely goes anywhere without Winona—and you really should meet Winona," Eloise told her.

"I appreciate the invitation," Charlotte said. "But I'm happy to spend a quiet night alone here, if you're sure you don't mind."

"Of course, we don't mind," Eloise said.

"And we won't be too late," Dante promised.

"Don't rush back on my account."

"What are you going to do for food?" Eloise asked, sounding worried.

"I get that you're a mother now," Charlotte said, "but you're not *my* mother and I'm perfectly capable of fending for myself."

"You're right. I'm sorry."

"You should save your apologies for Dante's parents when you show up late," Charlotte teased.

"We're not going to be late," Eloise said.

"We are if we don't leave right now," Dante told her.

"Leaving right now," she promised, sliding the strap of the mammoth diaper bag onto her shoulder and kissing her sister's cheek as she passed.

Dante carried the baby in her car seat. "The restaurant downstairs has good food. Order room service if you're hungry," he said, then he kissed Charlotte's cheek, too.

She was smiling as she closed the door behind them, happy that her sister had found a good man—and sad that she kept losing the same one.

Chapter Sixteen

Billy knew that he'd done the right thing. The necessary thing. So why did everything feel so wrong?

He tried to shake off his mood, to ignore the fact that—less than twenty-four hours after driving away from Charlotte—he missed her like crazy.

Well, he was going to have to get used to missing her, because it was already the twenty-third of December, which meant that she'd be leaving Bronco in just over a week and his chances of crossing paths with her in town would go from slim to nil.

He finished grooming Mocha and was leading the gelding back to his stall when he heard footsteps approaching.

"I stopped by your house first. Branson told me that I'd find you here."

He latched the stall door before turning to face Seth

Taylor. "Are you lost? Because you're a long way from the Triple T."

"I would have trekked twice as far if necessary to kick your ass."

If he had to guess, Billy would say that Seth's dander was up because he'd somehow found out that certain things had transpired between Billy and Charlotte since her return to town. But Billy wasn't foolish enough to bring up her name when her middle brother was obviously spoiling for a fight.

"You might want to think twice before barging into the middle of something that you know nothing about," he cautioned.

"I know that you hurt my sister. Eloise told me that Charlotte was crying. *Over you*."

Billy hated to think it might be true. He certainly hadn't intended to hurt Charlotte—he'd only wanted to protect his own heart.

"I didn't even realize you two were seeing each other," Seth continued, without giving Billy a chance to respond. "But since you obviously didn't learn your lesson about messing with her twenty years ago, I came by to give you a refresher."

"We weren't seeing each other," he said, determined to set the record straight. "Just occasionally having sex."

Seth's eyes narrowed. "You want me to punch you, don't you?"

Maybe he did.

Maybe he wanted an excuse to fight back—to burn off some of the frustration that churned in his gut. Some of the hurt that he wasn't quite ready to acknowledge.

Because acknowledging what he was feeling would require accepting that he had feelings for Charlotte, and he refused to believe it could be true. That he could have been so foolish as to have fallen for her again.

Far better to take whatever punishment her brother wanted to dish out than admit his own heart was battered and bruised.

"It wouldn't be the first time," he said to Charlotte's brother.

"No," Seth acknowledged. "The first time was when I found out you got her pregnant when she was only seventeen."

"I was seventeen, too."

"Which is the only reason I didn't beat you to a pulp."

"You didn't do nearly as much damage as she did when she trampled my heart."

Seth's gaze narrowed thoughtfully. "Is that what this is—payback because she left you at the altar all those years ago?"

"Of course not," he denied.

"I hope that's true," Charlotte's brother said. "Because she was a scared teenager when she walked out on your wedding. You're a grown man who shouldn't be holding a grudge two decades later."

Seth turned to leave then, and Billy made the mistake of letting down his guard. He even exhaled a sigh of relief.

"Just one more thing," Seth said, pivoting back again.

"What's that?" he asked warily.

Charlotte's brother responded to the question by slamming his fist into Billy's jaw.

* * *

He hung around the barn until Branson texted to let his dad know that he was heading into town with Nicky and Jill to do some shopping. Billy replied with a reminder to keep an eye on the weather, as snow was in the forecast, and his elder son promised to do so. When he saw his truck pass by the barn, Billy headed back to the house and found a bag of peas in the freezer to use as a makeshift ice pack.

"I am not in the mood for any more visitors today," he grumbled in response to the knock on his door.

But his family had never stood on ceremony, as his dad proved by opening the door and walking in.

"That looks like it hurts," Asa said, finding a mug in the cupboard and filling it with coffee.

"A little," Billy admitted.

His dad handed him the first mug, then poured a second for himself. "What happened?"

"I ran into a door."

"A door named Taylor?"

"Yeah."

"Seth, I'm guessing," Asa continued, in a conversational tone.

"Right again," he said.

"I thought it was his truck I saw parked by the barn a little while ago."

Billy cautiously wiggled his jaw before lifting the mug to his lips to sip the coffee.

"Did you hit him back?" his dad wanted to know.

He shook his head. "No."

"You were never one to start fights, but you usually finished them."

"It wasn't really a fight," Billy said.

"It doesn't sound like it," Asa agreed. "It sounds like Seth hit you and you let him walk away."

"Because I deserved it."

"It was about Charlotte, then," his dad guessed.

"I really don't want to talk about this."

"Which is a sign that you know you screwed up."

"I didn't screw up," he denied. "I did what needed to be done."

"Which is what?"

"End things before anyone got in too deep."

"I don't think you actually did," Asa remarked. "Because the expression on your face is darker than the clouds overhead."

Which only confirmed that his expression reflected his mood. "If I'm not feeling particularly jolly, it's because this will be our first Christmas since the divorce and I'm not exactly looking forward to spending it without my kids."

"I can understand that," his dad said. "Although the reality is, Branson is seventeen, so how many more years do you expect him to be home? Nicky and Jill aren't little kids anymore, either."

"I guess I just didn't expect things to change this quickly."

"One of the most bittersweet aspects of parenthood is guiding your children toward independence and then letting them go."

"So I'm starting to realize," Billy admitted.

"Another thing you should realize is that your house won't seem so empty when the kids are gone if there's someone else around."

"Did you have anyone particular in mind?" he asked dryly.

"That should be your choice." Asa held his son's gaze. "Yours and nobody else's."

Which, he realized, was his father's way of saying that if Billy chose to be with Charlotte, Asa would risk his wife's wrath to support his decision.

But Billy had already made a different choice: to let her go.

Charlotte refused to let Billy Abernathy ruin her holiday. No way was she going to mope around because her foolish heart was feeling a little bruised.

Okay, maybe it was more than a little bruised. But it wasn't the first time her heart had been broken, so she knew it would heal. It would take some time, but eventually she'd move on.

Getting over Billy was another matter. Because she knew now that she'd never quite managed to do that.

Which meant that there might be some awkward encounters between them if she decided to stay in Bronco, but she had to believe that the awkwardness would fade with time.

Still, she couldn't help but feel sad that she'd ruined the opportunity to be friends with him again by jumping his bones. Maybe if she'd been satisfied with meeting for the occasional cup of coffee and conversation, they would still be friends.

Except that after only one kiss, she'd known friendship wasn't what she wanted.

Not with Billy.

Why was it so hard for her to get over him?

Was the chemistry between them really so powerful that it had endured for more than two decades?

Or was it the sense of familiarity that had motivated her actions?

Or maybe simple nostalgia—the lingering memory of loving him when they were so much younger—that made her want to be with him again?

Whatever the reason, he'd made it clear that their recent intimate encounters were nothing more than that. They definitely weren't the foundation of the relationship that she'd believed they were building.

Perhaps it was ridiculous to think that she could have fallen head over heels in love with him again after only two weeks, and not even Charlotte really believed that was what had happened. No, the truth was, she'd never stopped loving Billy Abernathy.

Despite the fact that their lives had taken different paths two decades earlier, she'd continued to hold him in her heart. Even when she'd learned that he was planning to marry another woman. And when she'd heard that he'd had a baby with his new wife. And when they'd had a second child and even a third.

She'd been happy that he was happy—because that's what she'd always wanted for him. But she'd been envious, too. Envious that he'd found a way to have the life they'd always planned with someone else, while she remained alone, missing him and secretly yearning for the children she'd believed they would one day have together.

Most of the time, she'd managed to ignore that yearning. Because she had a good life—a full life—and it seemed selfish to want anything more. But since coming home to Bronco, that old yearning had started tugging at her again.

No doubt because she'd been spending so much time with Eloise and her sister's beautiful baby girl. Another contributing factor might have been seeing Billy with his kids and observing that he was as wonderful a father as she'd always suspected he would be.

But his kids were teenagers now, and she didn't imagine he'd want to start all over again. Certainly he didn't want to start over with her, as he'd proven by ending their fledgling relationship almost before it had begun.

Which was another reason she needed to get over him once and for all. Because if she was serious about having a baby—and if she was staying in town and working a regular job, it wasn't outside the realm of possibility—she needed to finally abandon any residual fantasies about her first love and move on.

But first, she had an errand to run.

"You've become one of my most valued customers," Sadie said, when Charlotte walked through the door of Holiday House the day before Christmas Eve.

"This was my favorite shopping spot when I was a kid, and I love it even more now," Charlotte told her.

"And I love to hear that," her new friend said.

She breathed in deeply, let the scents of apple cider

and gingerbread fill her soul with happy thoughts of Christmas.

"Lynda called to say that my wreaths were ready."

Sadie nodded. "I finished them yesterday afternoon. I'm so sorry I couldn't get to them sooner, but I was swamped with orders."

"Are you kidding? I was thrilled that you even had time to make them—not only in the midst of a busy Christmas season but also planning your wedding," Charlotte said.

Not to mention that her request had been a little out-of-the-ordinary. While she'd admired what Sadie could do with traditional flowers and holiday colors, Charlotte had asked for three beach-themed wreaths in colors that brought to mind turquoise waters and sandy beaches (possibly with shell-pink accents)—one for each of her full-time colleagues on the Dolphin Harbour Project. Thankfully, Sadie had been excited rather than daunted by the challenge, though she'd warned Charlotte that she might have to wait for the delivery of supplies before she could get started.

"It has been busy," Sadie agreed with a laugh. "But it seemed like perfect timing to us—and for our honeymoon, as the shop isn't very busy right after Christmas."

"Because you closed for almost a week last year," an elderly female customer grumbled.

"And we're going to be closed for a week again this year, Mrs. Ferris," Sadie warned the old woman.

"It was almost two weeks," Beth, another of the shop's clerks, said. "But I convinced Sadie that Lynda and I could hold down the fort while she's basking in the sunshine of Aruba with her new husband."

"Did you know that expression—*hold down the fort*—has been traced back to General William Tecumseh Sherman in 1864?" Mrs. Ferris asked.

"I did not." Beth steered the customer away from Sadie and Charlotte.

"Another interesting fact about Sherman is that…"

The interesting fact was lost as they moved out of earshot.

"He died on Valentine's Day," Sadie filled in.

Charlotte looked at her blankly.

"General Sherman," the shopkeeper explained. "Mrs. Ferris is a former history teacher, and I've heard her spiel about the general before."

"I thought she looked familiar, but it wasn't until you said her name that I realized she was my former history teacher."

"Mine, too," Sadie said with a grin. "Now, was there anything else you were looking for today or did you just come in for the wreaths?"

"I came in for the wreaths, but I don't mind taking a few minutes to browse around."

"Then I'll let you do that while I get your order."

She wandered through the shop, pausing in the milestone section where she'd found the "Baby's First Christmas" ornament for Merry on her last visit. There were also "First Christmas as Mr. & Mrs." and "New Home" ornaments, and she suspected she would be buying both for Eloise and Dante the following year.

She picked up the bride and groom ornament, noted their smiling faces.

"You're not feeling the holiday spirit, Charlotte Taylor."

She was so startled, she bobbled—and nearly dropped—the ornament in her hand. After carefully replacing it on the hook, she turned around to face an elderly woman. "Do I know you?"

"We've never met." The stranger extended an arm, bracelets jingling. "I'm Winona Cobbs. I used to write a syndicated advice column—Wisdom by Winona—but I gave that up several years back. Now it's the name of my shop, located near Bronco Ghost Tours, my great-grandson's business."

The old woman—the deep lines on her face attested to the fact that she was very old—was wearing a cherry-red winter coat unbuttoned over a purple sweater and lime-green leggings. A chunky silver chain hung around her neck with a teardrop-shaped pendant set with a pink stone marbled with gray.

"It's rhodonite," Winona said, rubbing her thumb over the stone.

"It's beautiful," Charlotte said.

"Rhodonite helps the wearer achieve emotional balance. It can aid in clearing away emotional wounds from the past and nurture love in the present." The old woman lifted the pendant over her head and offered it to Charlotte. "And it would look beautiful on you."

"Oh, no," Charlotte protested. "I couldn't—"

"You must," Winona said, her tone gentle but firm.

Charlotte bowed her head, allowing the necklace to be put on her.

"Beautiful," the old woman said again, with a satisfied nod.

It really was, Charlotte thought. And the weight of the stone between her breasts, against her heart, felt warm and comforting somehow.

Winona touched a hand to her arm. "You'll work it out."

"I'm sorry?"

"And so will he." The old woman winked. "Wear the necklace to the wedding."

How did this stranger know that she'd been invited to Sadie and Sullivan's wedding?

"I will," she promised.

"Merry Christmas, Charlotte."

"Merry Christmas to you, too," she said.

The old woman started to turn away, then pivoted back again. "Oh, one more thing—rhodonite can also stimulate fertility."

Winona winked then and continued on her way.

Leaving Charlotte stunned, staring after her.

She hadn't told anyone about her renewed desire for a baby. Not even her sister or her mother. So why would this stranger have commented about fertility?

"Is everything okay?" Sadie asked, when Charlotte made her way to the counter to pay for the wreaths she'd ordered.

"I'm not sure," she admitted.

"Did Winona say something to upset you?"

"No. She's just a little…spooky," she decided, for lack of a better term.

"Why don't we have a cup of tea?" Sadie suggested, taking Charlotte's arm and steering her to the back of the shop.

"I'm fine," she said. "And I'm sure you don't have time to babysit me."

"I have time for a cup of tea with a friend," Sadie said. "Both Beth and Lynda are here and they know where to find me if they need me."

While Sadie busied herself making the tea, Charlotte tried to shake off the uneasy feelings that lingered after her encounter with Winona.

"I know you said you're fine, but I'm starving," Sadie said, setting a tin of Danish butter cookies on the table.

Charlotte sipped her tea while the other woman helped herself to a cookie.

"Did Winona give you that necklace?"

"She did."

Sadie reached into her sweater and pulled out a similarly shaped pendant with a warm yellow stone in the center.

"She gave me this one, too."

"Is that what she does—walks around town giving out jewelry?"

Sadie laughed. "Among other things."

"What other things?"

"She's a self-proclaimed psychic—has a shop where she reads palms and tells fortunes."

"Does she make a living doing that?"

"A lot of people swear that she's legit," Sadie said.

"What do *you* think?"

"I certainly wouldn't be quick to disregard anything she said to me."

She thought about the psychic's cryptic words— *you'll work it out*—and wondered if the old woman could have been referring to Charlotte and Billy.

And if she had, Charlotte fervently hoped that she was right.

Chapter Seventeen

Billy was surprised to return to the house after completing his morning chores on Christmas Eve and find his daughter was already awake, sitting on the sofa, staring at the lights on the Christmas tree.

"I thought you were all about sleeping in because it's the holidays," he said.

"You know I can never sleep in on Christmas."

Of course, it wasn't really Christmas, but they were pretending it was because Branson, Nicky and Jill would be heading to their mom's later that night to wake up there on Christmas morning.

The prospect of being alone on Christmas Day wasn't a happy one for Billy, but he was doing his best to pretend that all was right with the world for the sake of his kids. And at least he'd have Sullivan Grainger's wedding to occupy a few hours the following day.

"I do know," he said, dropping a kiss on the top of her head. "Merry Christmas, Jilly Bean."

"Merry Christmas, Daddy."

The word filled his heart.

He was mostly "Dad" these days—proof that his little girl was growing up. But every once in a while, she slipped and called him "Daddy" again, just like she used to do.

"Did you peek at the tags on the presents under the tree?" he asked.

"Maybe."

"Who has the most?"

She rolled her eyes. "As if I didn't know that you'd make sure we all had the exact same number."

It wasn't something that he would have given much thought to, but Jane had impressed upon him the importance of equality. Some gifts might be bigger or smaller than others, but the kids would each have the same number of gifts, and he'd made sure to abide by the same rules.

"Your brothers still sleeping?" he asked.

"What do you think?"

"I think that you didn't make enough noise stomping down the stairs," he said with a wink.

"I *did* stomp," she assured him.

She'd always been the first one awake on Christmas Day. Aside from her parents, of course. Because while Billy went out to tend to the animals, Jane would be cooking bacon and eggs for breakfast.

He missed the comfort of those routines. And he missed the companionship. Or he had, in the beginning. But he'd gotten used to living on his own with the kids, going to sleep without someone beside him. And, in recent months, he'd decided that he preferred having the whole bed to himself.

Then he'd walked into the career fair at the high school and encountered Charlotte Taylor.

Had that really been less than two weeks earlier?

It seemed as if so much had happened in that brief span of time. So many highs and lows.

And while he didn't miss his ex-wife anymore, he was definitely missing Charlotte.

Nope. Not going there.

No point in wishing for what could never be.

Because Charlotte was gone, too.

He didn't think she'd actually left Bronco yet. As far as he knew, her plans to stay in town through the New Year hadn't changed. But she was gone from his life.

His choice, he reminded himself.

He'd let her go rather than give her another chance to break his heart.

So why did his heart feel broken anyway?

It was because the kids would be gone for Christmas. That was all, he told himself.

He was absolutely *not* twisted up over Charlotte Taylor.

"I need to get that turkey in the oven if we're going to eat sometime today."

"In that case, I'm going to go upstairs to get dressed," Jill decided.

"Don't be too quiet," Billy advised.

She grinned. "I wasn't planning to be."

* * *

When the boys finally got up, they had cinnamon rolls for breakfast before gathering around the tree to open their presents. There were some practical gifts, some fun gifts and, as always, the "most coveted" gift. For Jill, that was a puffy ski jacket; for Nicky, it was a couple of newly released video games; for Branson, it was a pair of AirPods.

When the packages were all opened and they were surrounded by a mountain of empty boxes and crumpled wrap, Branson got a trash bag and the kids began to stuff it with the discarded paper and ribbons.

It had been a good morning, Billy thought with satisfaction.

At least until Jill crawled under the tree to retrieve a bow that had ended up there and came out with an unopened present.

"Looks like we missed one," she said.

"It's nothing," Billy said quickly, reaching to take the gift from her.

But she'd already located the tag, as evidenced by the small pleat that formed between her brows.

"It's for Charlotte." She looked at her dad then. "What is it?"

"Nothing," he said again, snatching it from her hand and stuffing it into the trash bag Branson was still holding.

Now Branson and Nicky were looking at him, too.

Jill dug into the bag, searching for the discarded gift. She pulled it out and hugged it against her chest.

"You really like her, don't you, Dad?"

He rose from the sofa. "I need to check on the turkey."

"There's still more than three hours left on the timer," Branson told him.

"Then I'll start peeling the potatoes," he decided, turning toward the kitchen.

Jill stepped in front of him, blocking his path.

"Is it my fault?" Her eyes were filled with guilt and regret.

"Is what your fault?" he asked.

"Am I the reason that you stopped seeing Charlotte?"

"Absolutely not," he assured her.

"So what happened?" Nicky asked.

He really didn't want to do this.

He didn't want to talk to his kids about the implosion of his relationship with Charlotte. He didn't even want to think about it.

But of course they'd have questions.

Probably why a lot of divorced parents didn't bother to date—because it was so much more complicated than dating as a single person.

At least his kids hadn't had a chance to get attached to Charlotte. They didn't even know her very well and— with the exception of Jill in the beginning—he didn't think they liked her all that much.

"Things just didn't work out," he finally said in response to Nicky's question. "Sometimes things just don't work out."

"But could they?" Jill asked.

"What's with all the questions?" he asked wearily.

"You look sad," his daughter said.

Her brothers both nodded, looking solemn.

"I'm not sad," he told them. "How can I be sad when I'm celebrating Christmas with my three favorite people in the whole world?"

"I don't know, but you do," Jill insisted. "And I want to help you fix things so that you're not sad."

"I appreciate the thought, but what happened between me and Charlotte is between me and Charlotte. There's nothing you can do, Jilly Bean."

"But maybe there's something *you* can do," Branson said.

"I don't think so," he said. "And right now, I want to forget about all this other stuff and focus on enjoying the day together."

"I'm not sure we can do that," Nicky told him.

"Why not?"

"Because we're worried about you," Branson said.

"I promise you—there's no need to worry."

"We don't want you to be alone," Jill said.

"I'm not alone."

"We're not going to be here forever, Dad."

"Eventually we're going to go away to college and move on with our own lives," Nicky pointed out.

"And that's exactly how it should be," he agreed.

"Except me," Branson said. "I'm going to stay at the Bonnie B—but I'm not going to live with you forever."

"You're welcome to come back here, but you're going to college," Billy told his elder son.

"We're getting off topic," Jill complained, crossing her arms over her chest.

"And I really need to check on that turkey," Billy said.

"No, Dad," Nicky said, aligning himself with his

sister to block their dad's escape. "You need to work things out with Charlotte."

Billy looked at each of his kids in turn. "I didn't think you guys even liked Charlotte."

"We were just surprised to find out that you were dating her," Branson said.

"Yeah," Jill agreed. "But at least you were happy when you were with her."

"I was happy with Charlotte," he admitted. "But it was never going to last."

"How do you know?" his daughter prompted.

"Because she's a marine biologist in the Bahamas and I'm a rancher in Montana."

"Are there cattle ranches in the Bahamas?" Branson wondered.

"I have no idea," he admitted.

"You should look into it," Jill said.

"I'm not interested in ranching in the Bahamas," he said. "I don't want to be anywhere but right here—where you guys are."

"Maybe Charlotte could get a job here," Nicky suggested.

"I heard they're building a marine discovery center in Wonderstone Ridge," Jill said excitedly.

His sister Stacy had told him the same thing—and that there was a possibility Charlotte might be offered a position at the facility. But Charlotte's silence on the subject had convinced him that she had no interest in the possibility.

"I can't imagine she'd want to give up swimming

with dolphins to teach schoolkids about the ocean," he said gently to his daughter.

"She said talking to students is one of her favorite parts of the job, because we're the conservationists of the future."

"Maybe, instead of imagining what she might or might not want, you could actually ask her," Branson said.

Billy shook his head. "I'm not sure how I feel about taking dating advice from my kids."

"It's good advice," his elder son assured him.

"What do you know about women?" Billy challenged.

Branson's answering smirk reminded him that he needed to have a serious talk with his son—both of his sons, actually—about relationships and respect and responsibility.

But that could wait for another day.

First he needed to talk to Charlotte.

And maybe another conversation wouldn't change anything, but his kids were right. He had to at least try.

Maybe the marine discovery center was an option. He had no idea, because instead of talking to her, he'd walked away from her, too afraid of her potential answers to even ask the questions. Which only proved that his communication skills hadn't evolved much since he was seventeen years old.

Unfortunately, talking to Charlotte had to wait for another day, too, because today he wanted to focus on the time he had with his kids. Tomorrow was Christmas Day and he certainly had no intention of visiting her at the Triple T where her whole family—including Seth and his right hook—would be in attendance.

But he knew that she'd become friends with Sadie Chamberlin and been invited to Sadie and Sullivan's Christmas wedding. A wedding that he was conveniently planning to attend, too.

"Fine. I'll talk to Charlotte," he finally said to the kids.

"When?" Branson asked.

"Tomorrow."

"Why not today?" Nicky wanted to know.

"Because I've got a mountain of potatoes to peel before everyone gets here."

Nicky frowned. "Who's everyone?"

"Grandma and Grandpa and Aunt Stacy and Aunt Robin and Uncle Theo and Uncle Jace and Tamara and Frankie."

Jill's eyes went wide. "Everyone's coming here today?"

"When else were you going to celebrate Christmas with them?"

The kids seemed satisfied by that response—and happy to know that it was going to be Christmas as usual as much as possible.

"Can I get started on the potatoes now?" he asked them.

"I thought you were going to make me peel the potatoes," Branson said.

"I'm giving you the day off. Merry Christmas."

His elder son punched his fists in the air. "Woo hoo!"

Billy chuckled.

"Me, too?" Nicky asked hopefully.

He nodded. "Go try out those new games you got."

"I wanna play, too," Branson said, following his brother out of the room.

"Why don't you go with them?" he suggested to Jill, when she lingered.

"I don't like those kinds of games."

"So what do you want to do?"

"I can set the table," she said helpfully.

"I know you can, but what do you *want* to do?"

"I want to help you," she insisted. "Merry Christmas."

He punched the air like Branson had done. "Woo hoo!"

Despite the fact that her kids now ranged in age from thirty to forty-two, Imogen still hung all of their stockings on the mantel every year—and they were still the first thing opened on Christmas morning. There was never anything too fancy in the socks—usually some candy and novelties and gift cards to favorite shops. And this year there were two more stockings on the mantel—one for Dante and one for Merry.

They were having an early meal so that Dante and Eloise and Merry could then celebrate with the Sanchez family. An accommodation that surprised Charlotte, though she had no objection to the revised schedule, especially as it meant she wouldn't have to rush to get ready for Sadie and Sullivan's wedding.

So while the rest of her siblings were sprawled around the family room in a turkey coma, Charlotte was putting on a dress and touching up her makeup. She hadn't been sure about the pendant that Winona had given her, but she felt compelled to follow the old woman's advice and put it on—and was pleasantly surprised to discover how pretty the stone looked against the cranberry-colored fabric of the dress she'd borrowed from Eloise.

"Where are you off to?" Allison asked, when she found Charlotte donning her coat and boots.

"I'm going to a wedding."

Her sister wrinkled her nose. "Who gets married on Christmas?"

"The owner of Holiday House."

"Sadie Chamberlin's getting married?"

"How do *you* know Sadie?"

"Long before she took over Holiday House, we went to grade school together."

"Small world," Charlotte mused.

"Actually, the world's pretty big," Allison said. "It's only this town that's small."

"Do you want to come with me?"

"Thanks, but I'd rather stay here, drink wine and sing along with *White Christmas*."

"Ever notice that our holiday traditions seem much more fun when we add wine?"

"Or at least more tolerable," Allison said. "No wonder Eloise was in such a hurry to get out of here after dinner."

Charlotte hugged her sister. "I'll be back for *It's a Wonderful Life*."

"Just don't count on there being any wine left."

Charlotte suspected she was going to want a glass or two when she got back, because Sadie and Sullivan were exchanging vows at the same church from which she'd made her hasty escape twenty years earlier. And especially if she crossed paths with her almost-groom there today, which she knew was a distinct possibility.

But decorated as it was for the festive nuptials, with poinsettias on the altar and potted evergreen trees twinkling with white lights, the chapel bore little resemblance to the one from her wedding, when purple satin bows had adorned the pews and huge urns of purple flowers had flanked the altar.

Purple had never been Charlotte's favorite color, but the wedding planner, working within a tight time frame, had been given a lot of latitude to make her own decisions so long as the day was "absolutely perfect"—per the instructions from Thaddeus and Imogen.

And everything had been perfect—right up until the minute the bride went missing.

But Charlotte had no regrets about her actions that day. She'd done what she had to do under the circumstances. She did, however, have some regrets about a few things that had happened since she came back to town.

Not rekindling her relationship with Billy, because being with him again had exceeded all of her fantasies. But perhaps she should have been honest with him about what she wanted—not just a few nights in his bed but a future for them together.

Except that, at the time, she hadn't known it herself. She hadn't realized that she wanted a second chance for them until he'd nixed the possibility.

You don't know what you've got until it's gone...and I found out a little too late...

The lyrics to the old song—one of her mother's

favorites—echoed in the back of her head, taunting her. Because it had been true twenty years ago, and it was equally true now.

She touched the stone hanging between her breasts, wondering if it could really promote healing wounds of the past, as Winona had suggested?

If it could, maybe she should give it to Billy, as everyone seemed to think he was the one who'd been hurt the most by her decision. But just because she'd been the one to walk away from their wedding didn't mean it had been easy—even if it had been the right thing to do, for both of them.

Charlotte pushed aside the memories and settled in a seat near the back of the rapidly filling church.

Over the past few weeks, the town had been buzzing about the upcoming wedding, but it was Sadie herself who'd told Charlotte how she had fainted the first time she saw Sullivan Grainger because he looked so much like her sister's presumed dead ex-husband. Apparently Sullivan had managed to catch her before she crumpled to the ground, and when she'd come to, he'd been holding her in his arms.

It sounded like the perfect beginning to a holiday romance, Charlotte thought, and wondered if Susanna Abernathy might one day put Sadie and Sullivan's love story onstage at Bronco Theater. More important, though, that first meeting was the beginning of happily-ever-after for Sadie and Sullivan, and Charlotte was thrilled to witness their nuptials today.

When the music started, she looked to the front of the church where the very handsome groom stood beside his best man—his twin brother Bobby Stone. Then the matron of honor appeared. Charlotte recognized her as Everlee Abernathy, owner of Cimarron Rose, a boho clothing boutique located near Sadie's Holiday House.

Evy was wearing a gorgeous red velvet gown with long sleeves and carrying a bouquet of white roses and red peonies with accents of cedar, pine cones and berries. Evy's young daughter, Lola, came next, wearing a similar dress with a shorter skirt and carrying a pomander ball of white roses and red peonies.

Then the music changed and the guests all rose in anticipation of the appearance of the bride. Sadie did not disappoint. She was absolutely gorgeous in a long-sleeved A-line gown of Chantilly lace, carrying a slighter larger bouquet. At her side was her mother, who hugged both her daughter and soon-to-be son-in-law before taking her seat in the front row.

It was a beautiful winter wedding—with all of the festive touches anyone would expect from the proprietor of Holiday House—and Charlotte teared up a little when the bride and groom exchanged their vows. Though she hadn't known her new friend long and had only met Sullivan once, it was obvious in the way they looked at one another and the emotion in their voices when they promised to love one another "till death do us part" that they meant every word.

After the ceremony, when the guests were mingling in the community hall adjacent to the chapel, she was feeling proud of herself for hardly thinking about Billy at all—until she turned around and found herself face-to-face with him.

Chapter Eighteen

Damn, he looked good. Not only as handsome as ever but seemingly unaffected by their breakup. She, on the other hand, had barely slept in days and feared that the concealer she'd applied to the dark circles under her eyes wasn't living up to its name.

"Merry Christmas, Charlotte."

She had to swallow around the lump in her throat before she could reply. "Merry Christmas, Billy."

"It was a nice ceremony, don't you think?"

She nodded.

"And a surprisingly large crowd, considering it's Christmas Day."

She started to nod again, then shook her head instead, blinking to hold back the tears that threatened.

"You don't think it's a large crowd?"

"That's not what I mean."

"What did you mean?"

"I can't…" She shook her head again. "I can't do this, Billy."

"Do what?"

"Pretend we're just a couple of old friends catching up at a wedding."

"Aren't we old friends?" he asked gently.

"There was a time, not so long ago, when I thought—hoped—we were a lot more. But I guess I was the only one." She started to turn, to walk away, because she didn't want him to see that her heart was breaking all over again.

"No." He caught her arm, halting her retreat. "You weren't the only one."

Out of the corner of her eye, she saw one of the other guests elbow her date before gesturing to Charlotte and Billy. Another leaned close to whisper to a friend, then both turned to look in their direction.

Apparently their appearance here together, even though they weren't really together, was creating something of a stir.

"Maybe we should find a quieter place to talk," Billy suggested, proving that he wasn't oblivious to the scrutiny they were under.

"That might be a good idea," she agreed, following him to the coatroom.

But when they were alone, instead of picking up the thread of their conversation, he reached into his jacket pocket and pulled out a gift-wrapped box.

"This is for you."

"You got me a Christmas present?"

He nodded and thrust it toward her. "Open it."

She hesitated. "I don't think that's a good idea."

"Please," he said.

Though still reluctant, Charlotte took the package from him and did as he requested, wondering if he could see that her hands weren't quite steady as she tore the paper off the box.

She lifted the lid to reveal a crystal block laser-etched to depict three dolphins leaping out of the water.

"It's…beautiful," she said. "Thank you."

"I'm not very good with words sometimes," Billy acknowledged, "so I wanted to give you something—a symbol—to show you that I know what you'd be giving up if I asked you to stay in Bronco…with me."

Hope started to fill her heart—but she immediately trampled it down and lifted her head to meet his gaze.

"When were you going to ask me to stay? Before or after you broke up with me?"

He winced at the bluntness of her question. "Before. And after." He stuffed his hands into his pockets before expanding on his response. "I never wanted to break up with you, but I also didn't want to be the one left behind. Again.

"And when I found out that you'd been offered a job in Wonderstone Ridge, and that you hadn't said anything to me about it, I assumed you weren't interested in the position—or making your return to Bronco more permanent."

She rubbed her thumb over the crystal. "I was never actually offered a job in Wonderstone Ridge. I was only contacted about the possibility," she said, eager to clarify that fact. "But how did you hear about it?"

"Stacy was at the new baby store and overheard your sister talking to her boyfriend."

"And she immediately rushed back to the Bonnie B to tell you," Charlotte guessed.

"She thought I already knew. She assumed that it was the kind of news someone would share with the person they were involved with."

"I wanted to tell you," she confided now. "But I didn't want to put any pressure on our relationship or make you feel as if you had to make a decision about our future together just because I had the potential opportunity to stay in town."

"I guess I can understand that," he acknowledged.

"I think part of our miscommunication stems from the fact that we were both aware our relationship was supposed to have a time limit," she said. "When I first came home, I was only planning to stay in Bronco until the New Year—until the funding came through to continue my research. Which happened a few days ago."

"What does that mean?" Billy wondered.

"It means the Dolphin Harbour Project is funded through the next five years."

He considered that revelation for a minute before cautiously venturing to ask, "Does that impact your plans?"

She shook her head. "I've had some amazing experiences and visited some incredible places around the globe over the past twenty years, but I'm ready to put down roots now. And I want to do so here—in Bronco."

He sighed, obviously relieved by her response. "You

have no idea how happy it makes me to hear you say that…but I still have to wonder if you might someday regret giving up a career you obviously love."

"What I'm giving up is nothing compared to the possibility of a future with you," she assured him, then immediately worried that she might be moving too fast. "Or am I being too presumptuous? You said that you wanted to ask me to stay, but you haven't actually done so."

"You're not being too presumptuous," he said. "I do want you to stay, and there's nothing I want more than a future with you, too. Because I love you, Charlotte. I don't think I ever stopped loving you."

She had to blink away the happy tears that blurred her vision, because she wanted a clear picture of this moment to hold in her heart forever. "I love you, too. I always have and I always will."

Finally, he kissed her. It was a kiss of healing and hope and Charlotte knew that as long as she was in his arms, she was exactly where she wanted to be.

When he finally lifted his mouth from hers, he said, "When I woke up this morning, I was sure this was going to be the worst Christmas ever. Now, I think it has the potential to be one of the best."

"Only the potential?"

"If I could talk you into coming home with me, it would definitely top the list," he assured her.

She smiled. "Let's find the bride and groom, give them our best wishes and get out of here."

They made it to the Bonnie B in record time. Of course, there wasn't a lot of traffic on the roads, considering that it was Christmas Day. Or maybe they were simply in a hurry.

Only days had passed since Charlotte had last been at Billy's house, in his bed, but a lot had happened in those few days. Her emotions had been on a roller coaster of highs and lows, and she knew there would be a lot more of both in the future, but she felt confident that they could handle whatever might come their way, so long as they were together.

They were barely inside the door before he was kissing her again, and she was kissing him back with equal fervor—eager to make love with the man she loved and who loved her.

He was working the buttons of her coat when her phone pinged.

"I'm ignoring that," she told him.

"I've waited a long time for you—I can wait another minute while you respond to a text message," he promised.

So she pulled out her phone while he hung up their coats.

I'm opening another bottle of wine and starting the next movie.

"It's my sister," she told Billy.

"Eloise?"

"Allison."

She typed a quick reply:

Enjoy both. I'm not going to be home until very late. (Or maybe tomorrow ;))

Did you hook up at the wedding?!? Tacky!

NOT a wedding hookup... Billy.

Allison responded to that with a string of heart emojis.

Charlotte sent back xoxo.

"Everything okay?" Billy asked.

"Everything's very okay," she assured him, tucking her phone into the side pocket of her purse.

"Do you want a glass of wine? There's some of that pinot noir left from the other night."

She shook her head. "I don't want any wine. I only want you."

"Well, that's a lucky coincidence," he said. "Because I want you, too."

He lowered his head to kiss her again, but she put a hand on his chest, holding him back.

"There's something else you want to say," he realized.

"There is," she admitted. "But I'm afraid that what I want to say might spoil this perfect moment."

"Nothing's going to spoil this moment," he promised.

"What if I told you that I wanted to have a baby?"

He was silent for a long minute.

"I know you've been there, done that. You've got three teenagers," she said. "And I thought I'd given up on the idea of having a baby of my own. But seeing you with your kids and spending time with Merry... I realized that I hadn't given up on my longtime dream of being a mom, I'd just set it aside—for a really long time.

"And I don't know how easy or difficult it might be to conceive at this point in my life, but I want to try. I want to try to have a baby *with you*."

"I have to admit, I wasn't expecting anything like that," he finally said.

"Is it a deal breaker?" she asked cautiously.

Because if her only choice was between a life with Billy and never being a mom or a life without Billy, she'd choose him in a heartbeat. But it wasn't a choice she wanted to make.

"No," he decided, shaking his head for emphasis. "It might take me some time to get used to the idea of starting at square one again when I'm about to send my eldest kid off to college, but it's definitely not a deal breaker." He put his arms around her. "There are no deal breakers so long as I get to be with you."

"I feel exactly the same way," she told him.

He responded to that by lifting her into his arms and carrying her to the bedroom.

"I'm capable of walking, you know."

"I have no doubt," he said.

"Then why, every time we've been headed to your bedroom, have you picked me up and carried me?"

"Maybe I want to be sure you don't have a chance to change your mind."

"I'm not going to change my mind."

But they both knew it had happened before. Twenty years earlier, she'd agreed to marry him—and then she'd walked out on their wedding. And though they'd cleared the air about what happened that day, she realized he might still be wary of trusting her to stick around this time.

So when he lowered her to her feet beside the bed, she lifted her hands to frame his face, forcing him to meet her gaze.

"I'm not going to change my mind," she said again. "Not about you. Not about us. I understand why you might have trouble believing me, but I'm going to be here, every day, until you're finally convinced—and then every day after."

"It might be easier to convince me if you were naked," he said.

She smiled at that, then her smile faded. "I know I hurt you when I took off the way I did. But I need you to know that I left because I felt as if my life was spiraling out of my control and I was scared—not because I didn't love you."

"I know you loved me," he said, all teasing forgotten now. "I just always wondered if maybe you didn't love me enough."

She shook her head. "If anything, I loved you too much, and that was part of what scared me. But I'm not scared now," she told him. "And regardless of what happens with the job in Wonderstone Ridge, I'm not going anywhere."

"I'm very happy to hear it," he said.

"Now," she said, reaching for his belt, "we can move on to the naked portion of the evening."

Billy didn't need to be told twice.

He reached behind her to unzip her dress, then pushed the fabric over her shoulders and down her arms. The garment pooled at her feet, leaving her clad in a black lace bra, matching panties and thigh-high, stay-up stockings.

"I didn't think there was anything sexier than you in simple cotton," he said. "I might have been wrong."

"The new lingerie was an early Christmas present to myself that I hoped you might also enjoy. And even though I didn't expect to end up back here tonight, I decided the occasion warranted it. Plus I've discovered that I like the way lace feels against my body."

"I like the way lace feels against your body, too," he said, tracing a fingertip along the scalloped edge of one of the stockings. "Very much so."

Then his hands skimmed up her torso, to the pendant nestled between her breasts.

"Was this another Christmas present?" he asked, lifting the stone for a closer look.

"A before-Christmas present," she said. "From Winona Cobbs."

"And what kind of mystical powers did she claim it possesses?" he asked, proving that he was familiar with the old woman—or at least her reputation.

"She said it can aid in clearing emotional wounds from the past and nurture love in the present…and that it could stimulate fertility." And maybe it was silly to believe the stone could do any of those things, but Charlotte was thirty-seven years old and if she was going to have a baby, she'd take all the help she could get.

"Then I guess we better leave it on," he said.

"You're really okay with the idea of having another baby?"

"With you, yes," he said.

"Of course, it might not happen—and probably not as easily as it did twenty years ago."

"Which is a good reason to start trying right now and keep trying until we get the result we want."

She smiled. "That sounds like a very good plan to me."

A long time later, when they were snuggled together under the covers and drifting toward sleep, Billy's phone buzzed.

He reluctantly eased away from her to dig it out of the pocket of his jeans.

"Is everything okay?" she said.

"Yeah." He sighed. "The kids hated the idea of me being alone for the whole of Christmas Day, so they convinced their mom to bring them home tonight."

"I should get back to my parents' place, too," she said.

"I'm sorry."

"Don't apologize for having great kids."

"They are pretty great," he agreed. "But right now, their timing sucks."

"It would have been a lot worse if they'd texted an hour ago," she pointed out. "Or not texted at all."

"I really don't want you to go."

"I don't want to go, either," she said. "But I don't think Branson, Nicky and Jill would be too happy to come home and find me in your bed, because the last time, they weren't too happy to find me here at all."

"There have been a lot of changes in their lives over the past few months," he noted. "I'm sorry they took it out on you."

"I understand. I just hope that they eventually warm to the idea of you and me together."

"They already have," he told her. "Because they know that you make me happy."

"Do you think a cat would make them even happier?"

"A cat?" he echoed dubiously.

"Dante, Eloise's boyfriend, has been taking care of a stray cat for the past several weeks. Actually, his parents have been taking care of it since he moved into the hotel. But I was thinking, now that I'm going to be putting down roots in Bronco, I could take the cat off his hands, and he agreed it sounded like a good idea."

"What kind of cat?" Billy asked.

"Why does it matter what kind of cat?"

"Because my brother Jace has been trying to track down an orange tabby that belonged to Frankie's birth mother."

"Dante's cat is an orange tabby…which makes me think it's not really Dante's cat." Charlotte pouted just a little. "I guess I'm not going to get a cat after all."

"If you've got your heart set on a feline companion, I'm sure your cousin Daphne could help you find one at Happy Hearts," he said, naming the local animal sanctuary.

"That's something to think about," she agreed. "But the only thing my heart is really set on is you."

He brushed his lips over hers. "I'm all yours."

Epilogue

It was difficult to believe that, only a week earlier, Charlotte had been headed to Sadie and Sullivan's wedding on her own, her future in Bronco uncertain.

Since then, she'd spent every possible minute with Billy—and his kids, when they were around. Of course, she went back to the Triple T every night, because although Branson, Nicky and Jill seemed happy enough to let her hang around, she wanted to give them time to get used to seeing her at the dinner table before they had to face her over breakfast.

She'd also met with Sean McCaffrey and agreed to take the position of educational director at the new marine discovery center in Wonderstone Ridge. She'd been walking on air when she left that meeting—and crying when she called her boss at the Dolphin Harbour Project. He'd told her that she'd be missed, but she knew that there were plenty of qualified and eager candidates for her job and it wouldn't take him long to replace her—especially now that their funding had been secured.

It had, indeed, been a year of changes, and now she was headed to the Bonnie B to ring in the New Year with Billy and his family. When she arrived, she was surprised to discover that there were several other vehicles already in the driveway.

"Branson's buddies," Billy responded to her question about all the cars. "Jill has a friend here, too, but she's not old enough to drive. And Nicky's hanging out with his online pals."

"New Year's Eve party at your house, I see."

"It's not really a party."

"There are eight teenagers in your house."

"Anything less than a dozen isn't really a party."

She chuckled at his logic.

"And anyway," he said, drawing her into his arms, "I figured if the kids were preoccupied with their friends, they'd be less likely to notice if we snuck out for a little while."

"Where are we sneaking out to?"

"Just for a short walk."

"It's December thirty-first. Winter in Montana."

"It's winter in the Bahamas, too," he pointed out to her.

"But winter in the Bahamas is seventy-five degrees, not fifteen."

"Is it really your plan to stay indoors for the next several months?"

"As much as possible," she confirmed.

"Well, I'm asking you to indulge me tonight," he said.

"Fine." She shoved her feet back into her boots and let him help her with her coat. Then she added a hat and mittens (Christmas gifts from Eloise) because, short walk or not, it was cold outside.

Billy slung his arm across her shoulders, holding her close to protect her from the wind as they headed away from the house. A few minutes later, he muscled open the door of the barn and ushered her inside.

"Now I'm thinking that your intention was a roll in the hay rather than a walk."

He chuckled. "An intriguing thought, but I don't want to be away from the house too long."

"You don't think we could be quick?"

"I don't want to rush through a single minute of the time we have together."

She sighed. "You're pretty good with words when you want to be, cowboy."

"Hold that thought," he said. "And...cover your eyes."

"Why?"

"Please."

Though his response didn't answer her question, she dutifully lifted her mitten-clad hands and placed them over her eyes.

Billy put his arm around her waist and guided her past a row of horse stalls—having been raised on a ranch, she was familiar with the scents and the sounds of animals bedded down for the night—before unlatching a gate.

"You can look now," he said.

She dropped her hands away and found herself facing a collage of photographs—pictures of herself and Billy from kindergarten through high school graduation—spread over several poster boards propped up on a pyramid of hay bales.

"This is...wow." She took a step forward, into the vacant stall, to more closely examine the pictures. "Where did you dig up all these old photos? And when did you have time to do this?"

"Most of the photos were in boxes in my parents' attic. The kids helped me sort through them and arrange the display."

"We had quite the history together, didn't we?" she mused, taking off her mittens and stuffing them into the pockets of her coat.

"We did," he agreed. "But I didn't bring you out here to reminisce about the past. I wanted to talk about the future."

"I know you—and Branson, Nicky and Jill—have been through a lot in the past several months," she said. "And I'm happy to take things slow."

"That seemed to make the most sense to me, too," he acknowledged. "To ease the kids into getting used to you being around. Apparently they don't need to be eased."

"What are you saying? That it's okay if I leave a toothbrush in your bathroom?" She was trying not to jump too far ahead, for fear that she might be disappointed.

"I'm saying that you can leave all your stuff wherever you want around the house."

"Are you asking me to move in with you?" she asked him cautiously.

"No. Well, yes. Kind of." He sighed. "I warned Jill that I'd mess this up."

"Mess *what* up?" Charlotte asked cautiously.

He drew her a few steps back from the collage. "Can you see it now?"

Her breath caught in her throat, because she could.

Now that she wasn't looking closely at any individual photo, she could see that the pictures had been arranged on the poster boards to create letters—and those letters spelled out WILL YOU MARRY ME?

She had to blink away the tears that filled her eyes to focus on him. "Are you sure—"

Before she could even finish the question, Billy held up a gorgeous diamond solitaire engagement ring that he'd pulled out of his pocket.

Apparently he was very sure.

"I know you've only been back in Bronco a few weeks," he acknowledged. "But I've already spent more than twenty years of my life without you, and I don't want to live without you any longer. So yes, I'm sure, and yes, I'm asking… Charlotte Taylor, will you marry me?"

She wanted to say "yes," too. She wanted to shout the word loud and clear, because she had no doubt that he was offering her everything she wanted. But she felt compelled to remind him, "You've barely been divorced a month."

"I've loved you forever," he said.

The simple words filled her heart to overflowing.

"Which is exactly as long as I've loved you," she told him.

"Is that a *yes*?"

"Your kids are really okay with this?"

"They helped me set all this up," he reminded her.

"In that case, my answer is a very definite *yes*," she confirmed.

He pressed his lips to hers then, sealing their bargain with a kiss.

"You know, I'm almost disappointed that I didn't have to bribe you," he said, as he slid the ring over her knuckle.

She glanced at the sparkling diamond. "There isn't anything you could offer me that I'd want more than your ring on my finger."

"Not even this?" he asked, reaching into the other pocket of his jacket and pulling out—

She had to laugh. "You were going to bribe me with Little Debbie Swiss Rolls?"

"I was going to promise to give you all of my snack cakes, every day, for the rest of our lives together if you agreed to be my wife."

"A tempting offer," she said. "But not nearly as tempting as the promise of spending the rest of our lives together."

"So what am I supposed to do with these now?" he asked.

She took the package out of his hand and tore it open. "We can share them."

"But only if you get the bigger one, right?" he teased.

"You said there isn't a bigger one."

"Well, if there is, I'll let you have it," he said.

"And that's only one of the reasons I love you."

As they fed one another bites of cake in-between long, lingering kisses, an orange tabby wandered into the barn, winding around their legs and mewing for attention. Neither of them noticed. Even when Charlotte heard someone calling for the cat from a distance, she was too busy kissing her fiancé to care.

"Whoops!" Jace realized he'd stumbled upon a private moment as soon as he walked into the barn in search of his AWOL feline.

"Take your cat and get out," Billy told his brother, not looking away from the woman in his arms.

"I'm going." Jace grinned as he scooped up the animal. "But first, I just want to say that I'm happy to see Morris isn't the only one who finally found his way home."

* * * * *

COMING NEXT MONTH FROM

◆ HARLEQUIN
SPECIAL EDITION

#3025 A TEMPORARY TEXAS ARRANGEMENT
Lockharts Lost & Found • by Cathy Gillen Thacker

Noah Lockhart, a widowed father of three girls, has vowed never to be reckless in love again...until he meets Tess Gardner, the veterinarian caring for his pregnant miniature donkey. But will love still be a possibility when one of his daughters objects to the romance?

#3026 THE AIRMAN'S HOMECOMING
The Tuttle Sisters of Coho Cove • by Sabrina York

As a former ParaJumper for the elite air force paramedic rescue wing, loner Noah Crocker has overcome enormous odds in his life. But convincing no-nonsense bakery owner Amy Tuttle Tolliver that he's ready to settle down with her and her sons may be his toughest challenge yet!

#3027 WRANGLING A FAMILY
Aspen Creek Bachelors • by Kathy Douglass

Before meeting Alexandra Jamison, rancher Nathan Montgomery never had time for romance. Now he needs a girlfriend in order to keep his matchmaking mother off his back, and single mom Alexandra fits the bill. If only their romance ruse didn't lead to knee-weakening kisses...

#3028 SAY IT LIKE YOU MEAN IT
by Rochelle Alers

When former actress Shannon Younger comes face-to-face with handsome celebrity landscape architect Joaquin Williamson, she vows not to come under his spell. She starts to trust Joaquin, but she knows that falling for another high-profile man could cost her her career—and her heart.

#3029 THEIR ACCIDENTAL HONEYMOON
Once Upon a Wedding • by Mona Shroff

Rani Mistry and Param Sheth have been besties since elementary school. When Param's wedding plans come to a crashing halt, they both go on his honeymoon— as friends. But when friendship takes a sharp turn into a marriage of convenience, will they fake it till they make it?

#3030 AN UPTOWN GIRL'S COWBOY
by Sasha Summers

Savannah Barrett is practically Texas royalty—a good girl with a guarded heart. But one wild night with rebel cowboy Angus McCarrick has her wondering if the boy her daddy always warned her about might be the Prince Charming she's always yearned for.

YOU CAN FIND MORE INFORMATION ON UPCOMING HARLEQUIN TITLES, FREE EXCERPTS AND MORE AT HARLEQUIN.COM.

HSECNM1123

Get 3 FREE REWARDS!

We'll send you 2 FREE Books plus a FREE Mystery Gift.

FREE
Value Over
$20

Both the **Harlequin® Special Edition** and **Harlequin® Heartwarming™** series feature compelling novels filled with stories of love and strength where the bonds of friendship, family and community unite.